NEW PENGUIN SHAKESPEARE
GENERAL EDITOR: T.J.B. SPENCER
ASSOCIATE EDITOR: STANLEY WELLS

WILLIAM SHAKESPEARE

✳

OTHELLO

EDITED BY
KENNETH MUIR

PENGUIN BOOKS

PENGUIN BOOKS

Published by the Penguin Group
Penguin Books Ltd, 27 Wrights Lane, London W8 5TZ, England
Penguin Books USA Inc., 375 Hudson Street, New York, New York 10014, USA
Penguin Books Australia Ltd, Ringwood, Victoria, Australia
Penguin Books Canada Ltd, 10 Alcorn Avenue, Toronto, Ontario, Canada M4V 3B2
Penguin Books (NZ) Ltd, 182–190 Wairau Road, Auckland 10, New Zealand

Penguin Books Ltd, Registered Offices: Harmondsworth, Middlesex, England

This edition first published in Penguin Books 1968
Reprinted with revised Further Reading
and Account of the Text 1996
3 5 7 9 10 8 6 4 2

Set in Ehrhardt Monotype
Printed in England by Clays Ltd, St Ives plc

CONTENTS

INTRODUCTION

Othello was written between 1602 and 1604, soon after *Hamlet* and not long before *King Lear*. It was performed at Court, not necessarily for the first time, in the autumn of 1604. Shakespeare found the plot in Giraldi Cinthio's collection of tales, *Hecatommithi* (1565); and his departures from his source throw light on his dramatic purpose.

Cinthio's is a sordid, melodramatic tale of sexual jealousy, and at first sight it may seem strange that Shakespeare should have been attracted by it. The heroine, called Disdemona, does not elope with the Moor (whose name is not given); her family agree to the marriage, though with some reluctance; and the couple live together in great happiness in Venice. The Moor is appointed to the command in Cyprus (Cinthio makes no mention of the Turkish danger). The Moor and his wife travel on the same boat. The villain's sole motive for his actions is his unsuccessful love for Disdemona, for which he blames the Captain (Shakespeare's Cassio). His plot is directed not against the Moor, but against Disdemona; and he is sexually, but not professionally, jealous of the Captain. The latter draws his sword upon one of the guard. He is not made drunk by the Ensign and there is no Roderigo. The Ensign steals the handkerchief while Disdemona is caressing his child. The Captain finds it in his house and, knowing it to be Disdemona's, he tries to return it; but he leaves hurriedly on hearing the Moor's voice. The murder of Disdemona is carried out by the villain and the Moor together: they knock her senseless with a sandbag

7

and make the roof fall, so as to make the deed look like an accident. Finally, the Moor is killed by Disdemona's kinsmen. The Ensign is tortured to death for another crime; and his wife was privy to the whole story. We have some pity for his victim, but no sympathy for the Moor.

There are several points in Cinthio's tale which may have fired Shakespeare's imagination. Jealousy was a theme to which he returned again and again, farcically in *The Merry Wives of Windsor*, tragi-comically in *Much Ado about Nothing* (where Claudio is deluded by a villain into believing Hero is unchaste), and he was later to deal with the subject again in the plays of his last period: in *Cymbeline* Posthumus is tricked by a villain into believing his wife has committed adultery; and in *The Winter's Tale*, where Leontes's jealousy of Hermione is self-begotten. In all these plays, as in Cinthio's story, the suspected woman is innocent. Then it was obvious that the misalliance of a white woman with a Moor offered dramatic opportunities; and the repentance of the Moor after the murder:

> *It came about that the Moor, who had loved the lady more than his very eyes, felt his loss and began to suffer so much longing for her that he went about like one out of his mind, looking for her in all sorts of places in the house*

would suggest the tragedy of the man who kills the thing he loves. Above all, perhaps, Cinthio's description of the Ensign:

> *although he was a most detestable character, nevertheless with high-sounding words he concealed the malice he bore in his heart, in such a way that he showed himself outwardly like another Hector or Achilles*

would chime with one of Shakespeare's obsessive themes – the contrast between appearance and reality, and the difficulty of distinguishing between the two. Claudio, confronted with the evidence of Hero's unchastity, exclaims:

> *Out on thee! Seeming! . . .*
> *You seemed to me as Dian in her orb.*

Isabella, in *Measure for Measure*, determines to unmask the 'seeming' of Angelo. Troilus finds it difficult to believe that the Cressida who capitulates to Diomed is the same person as the one he had loved. Hamlet discovers that one may smile and be a villain. Henry V's chief complaint of the conspirators against him was their hypocrisy. The villain in Cinthio's tale, whose persona was accepted by all his associates as his real character, posed the question of 'seeming' in its extreme form. It has been suggested that the question had a professional interest to Shakespeare. If an actor could play the role of a saint or even a woman so as to convince an audience, how was it possible to tell in real life whether a man was what he seemed? Iago, in a sense, is the apotheosis of the actor.

To transform the melodramatic story into tragedy necessitated a number of important changes. First, the character of the Moor, if it was to arouse tragic sympathy, had to be invested with nobility and greatness. This Shakespeare achieved primarily by the poetry he gave him to speak, which characterizes him as noble, magnanimous, royal, exotic, and (some critics believe) egotistical. Then Shakespeare added the threat to Cyprus by the Turks to show Othello's indispensability to the Venetian state: as even Iago admits,

> *Another of his fathom they have none*
> *To lead their business.*

The background of Othello's life is filled in, partly by his autobiographical account of his 'travels' history' and partly

9

by references throughout the play to incidents in his past life, from the death of his brother at his side, recounted by Iago, to the slaying of the malignant Turk in Aleppo. Most important of all is the way Shakespeare convinces us that Othello never ceases to love the bride he murders: he does not merely allow the love to be revived after the murder. Othello commits the murder himself and he executes justice on himself as soon as he knows that Desdemona was innocent.

Secondly, Shakespeare rejected the simple motivation of Cinthio's villain and made Iago direct his hatred, not against Desdemona, but against the Moor.

Thirdly, he invented the character of Roderigo, 'a gull'd Gentleman' as he is called in the Folio Dramatis Personae. He seems to have taken a hint from his own *Twelfth Night*, where Sir Toby Belch extracts money from Sir Andrew Aguecheek by promising to arrange for his marriage to Olivia, just as Iago promises Desdemona to Roderigo. Desdemona's marriage threatens to cut off Iago's supply of money from his dupe, and he therefore holds out the promise that she will take a lover – and this suggests to Iago the accusation of Cassio.

Fourthly, Shakespeare altered the character of Cassio. In Cinthio's tale he is wounded after supping with a prostitute. Shakespeare softens this by making the relationship between Cassio and Bianca less mercenary. He gives the handkerchief not to the *donna* in his lodgings – usually translated 'wife', though this is not necessarily Cinthio's meaning – but to Bianca. This tightens the structure, eliminates an inessential character, and gives Iago a useful instrument for arousing Othello's fury. The brawl which leads to the Captain's dismissal is not engineered by Cinthio's villain. Shakespeare reduces the element of chance by making Iago incite Roderigo to brave Cassio,

by making Cassio have a poor head for drinking, by making
Iago suggest to Cassio that he should ask Desdemona to
intercede for him, and by making Cassio privy to Othello's
courtship of Desdemona.

Fifthly, Shakespeare alters the way in which Iago gets
possession of the handkerchief. In the source, as we have
seen, the villain steals the handkerchief from Desdemona's
girdle while she is fondling his child. Shakespeare may
have altered this incident so that he could dispense with
the child, or because the Iago he had created would not
have had a child. The incident he substituted for it is at
first sight less plausible: Desdemona drops the handkerchief and Emilia picks it up and gives it to Iago. It has
been argued that this change turns accident into design.
She forgets about the handkerchief, which she prizes as
Othello's first gift to her, only at the moment when she is
worried about his headache. Her forgetfulness is in the
circumstances a sign of her love, not of carelessness.

Sixthly, Shakespeare alters the character of Emilia. Cinthio makes the villain's wife privy to his plot, but afraid
to reveal it. Emilia, though she steals the handkerchief, is
deceived, like everyone else, by her husband; and she turns
against him as soon as she learns the truth.

It has been suggested that Shakespeare's treatment of
the plot was influenced by a tale in Geoffrey Fenton's
Certaine Tragicall Discourses (1567), in which a foreign
soldier, an Albanian captain, kills his innocent wife out of
jealousy. The wife bewails her 'wretched fortune' but continues to love her husband; the Captain, when about to
stab his wife, 'embraced and kissed her, in such sort as
Judas kissed our Lord the same night he betrayed him',
as Othello kisses Desdemona; the wife's confession to God
is cut short by her want of breath; and the Captain, like
Othello, commits suicide, commending his soul 'to the

reprobate society of Judas and Cain'. If Shakespeare was influenced by Fenton's tale, it would lend some support to those who believe that there is an allusion to Judas's kiss of betrayal in Othello's last speech.

We are on more certain ground in supposing that Shakespeare went to Lewkenor's translation of Cardinal Contarini's *Commonwealth and Government of Venice* for some of his information about the Venetian state and that he made copious use of Philemon Holland's translation of Pliny's *Natural History* for filling in the exotic background of Othello's career. The Anthropophagi and other details of his defence before the senate, the simile of the Pontic Sea, and the reference to chrysolite are the most striking examples.

Richard Burbage, the leading actor in Shakespeare's company, played the part of the 'grieved Moor' and it was one of his greatest successes. We are told by Shakespeare's neighbour, Leonard Digges, that audiences were bored with Jonson's tragedies:

> *They prized more*
> *Honest Iago, or the jealous Moor.*

After the Restoration the play was attacked by Thomas Rymer for its improbabilities and for its failure to satisfy the demands of poetic justice. He concluded that the play was 'a bloody farce without salt or savour'; that the character of Iago was incredible because soldiers are genuinely honest; that the morals to be drawn from it are to warn 'all maidens of quality, without their parents' consent', not to run away with blackamoors, to warn 'all good wives, that they look well to their linen', and a warning to husbands 'that before their jealousy be tragical, the proof may be mathematical'. But Rymer's most serious complaint is that the innocent Desdemona is murdered:

What instruction can we make out of this catastrophe? Or whither must our reflection lead us? Is not this to envenom and sour our spirits, to make us repine and grumble at Providence, and the government of the world? If this be our end, what boots it to be virtuous?

Few later critics have taken Rymer's complaints seriously. But there have been several who have felt uneasy about the conclusion. Johnson found the last scene unendurable; Bradley thought the play evoked feelings of depression; and Granville-Barker declared that it was a tragedy without meaning. It is not merely that an innocent woman is murdered – for Lady Macduff and Cordelia are as innocent and Ophelia's fate is equally undeserved – but that the hero himself is degraded and destroyed by the villainy of his subordinate. It will be necessary to examine in some detail the characters of Iago and Othello to see how far these feelings of disquiet are justifiable.

Some actors playing the part of Iago make him into such an obvious villain that he deceives no one; but the essential thing about him, as of Cinthio's villain, is that he appears to be honest. That is the point of the iteration of *honest* and *honesty* right down to the moment of his unmasking. He deceives not merely Othello and Cassio, but Montano, Lodovico, and even Emilia. Even Roderigo, indeed, who knows Iago is not honest, does not at first suspect that he himself is being duped.

One actor who realized how the part should be played was Bensley, whom Charles Lamb described as

the only endurable one which I remember to have seen. No spectator, from his action, could divine more of his artifice than Othello was supposed to do. His confessions in soliloquy alone put you in possession of the mystery. There were no by-intimations to make the audience fancy their own

> *discernment so much greater than that of the Moor. The*
> *Iago of Bensley did not go to work so grossly. There was a*
> *triumphant tone about the character, natural to a general*
> *consciousness of power; but none of that petty vanity*
> *which chuckles and cannot contain itself upon any little*
> *successful stroke of its knavery – as is common with your*
> *small villains, and green probationers in mischief. It did not*
> *clap or crow before its time. It was not a man setting his*
> *wits at a child, and winking all the while at other children,*
> *who are mightily pleased at being let into the secret; but a*
> *consummate villain entrapping a noble nature into toils*
> *against which no discernment was available, where the*
> *manner was as fathomless as the purpose seemed dark, and*
> *without motive.*

Apart from the last two words of this description, to which
we shall have occasion to return, Lamb's account of Bensley's performance shows that the actor had precisely the
right conception of the part. It was followed by Edwin
Booth, the American actor, of whose Iago we are told
that 'if Othello had suddenly turned upon him, at any
moment in their interview, he would have seen only the
grave, sympathetic, respectful, troubled face that was com-
posed for him to see'. He advised any actor playing the
part to 'try to impress even the audience with your sincerity . . . Iago should appear to be what all but the
audience believe he is.' A great actor of our own day, Sir
Ralph Richardson, played the part in the same way. If
Iago is played as an obvious villain, Othello and the other
characters are reduced to credulous fools, whereas Shakespeare, as we have suggested, was concerned with the
difficulty of distinguishing between appearance and reality,
with the impossibility of detecting an absolute hypocrite.

Lamb, as we have seen, accepts Coleridge's view that

Iago's malignity was motiveless. It was accepted, too, by
Hazlitt, Swinburne, Bradley and Granville-Barker and by
many other critics, who assume that he loves evil for its
own sake, that he has said, with Satan, 'Evil be thou my
good', and that the various motives he acknowledges are
mere rationalizations. The Ensign of Shakespeare's source,
as we have seen, is motivated simply by his hatred of
Disdemona, arising from his thwarted lust. This motive is
mentioned by Iago only once. In addition to this motive
taken from Cinthio, Shakespeare provides several more,
presented with equal casualness, and seldom referred to
more than once. In the first scene Iago tells Roderigo that
he hates Othello for choosing Cassio, rather than himself,
as his Lieutenant; but this motive is not directly mentioned
after the first scene of the play, except once, casually, in the
soliloquy at the end of the Act:

> To get his place and to plume up my will
> In double knavery.

Even his desire to get Cassio's place fades into the background, though we are later reminded of it by Emilia in
the lines:

> I will be hanged if some eternal villain,
> Some busy and insinuating rogue,
> Some cogging, cozening slave, to get some office,
> Have not devised this slander. . . .

In his first soliloquy (I.3.377–82) Iago mentions another
motive, that Othello is 'thought abroad' to have seduced
Emilia. This is mentioned again in his second soliloquy
(II.1.286–7) with the addition that he also suspects Cassio
of cuckolding him. Neither of these motives is mentioned
again. Iago's ultimate motives for getting Roderigo to murder Cassio are not mentioned until the last Act (V.1.11–22)–

that Othello may reveal Iago's accusations to him, and that

> *He hath a daily beauty in his life*
> *That makes me ugly.*

It is not, therefore, surprising that Coleridge should describe one of the soliloquies as 'the motive-hunting of a motiveless malignity'.

Yet, from the nature of Iago's role, he cannot reveal himself except in soliloquy; and there are no soliloquies in Shakespeare's plays – or, indeed, in any Elizabethan plays – which do not express the genuine feelings or beliefs of the characters speaking them. We ought, therefore, to be suspicious of everything that Iago says to another person, unless it is afterwards corroborated, and to accept what he says in soliloquy, not of course as true, but as the expression of his actual feelings.

The soliloquy at the end of Act I is, in fact, a displaced aside in which Iago removes the mask for the first time: it throws a retrospective light on his dialogues with Roderigo. The marriage of Othello and Desdemona has come as a shock to Iago, because it threatens to cut off his main source of income. Since he can no longer get paid by Roderigo for assisting his suit with Desdemona, he has to convince his dupe that he hates Othello and that he will assist Roderigo to seduce Desdemona. As a proof of his hatred, he mentions the way Cassio has obtained the lieutenantship he thought that he himself deserved; and he shows this hatred in action by the foul images he uses about Othello's marriage in awakening Brabantio. It is significant that only Iago and Brabantio seem to have any colour prejudice against Othello. In the third scene Iago, anxious to persuade Roderigo that Desdemona is still attainable, assures him that when her lust for the Moor is sated she will find it 'as acerbe as the coloquintida' and she will turn to a younger man. Up to this point in the play the audience may assume that Iago hates Othello for his appointment of Cassio, that he hates Cassio for the same reason, that he is pretending loyalty to Othello for his own ends, and that he purports to have the lowest opinion of Desdemona's motives in marrying a coloured man. Then he is left alone; and before he begins to frame his plot against Othello he reveals his suspicion that he has been cuckolded (lines 380–84):

> I hate the Moor,
> And it is thought abroad that 'twixt my sheets
> He's done my office. I know not if 't be true
> But I, for mere suspicion in that kind,
> Will do as if for surety.

It is noteworthy that Iago does not say he hates the Moor *because* the latter has cuckolded him, or even because people think it, but that he hates the Moor, '*and* it is thought abroad . . .'. Bernard Spivack stresses the significance of the conjunction as 'The seam between the drama of allegory and the drama of nature, as well as between the kind of motivation proper to each'. In other words, Iago is both a stage devil, deriving ultimately from the Vice of the Morality plays, and a character in a more sophisticated Elizabethan tragedy. He hates goodness, at the same time as he has psychological motives for hating Othello.

We have some confirmation, not of the truth of Iago's suspicion, as some critics have absurdly supposed, but of the fact that he had indeed suspected his wife in Emilia's words in Act IV (2.144-6):

> Some such squire he was
> That turned your wit the seamy side without
> And made you to suspect me with the Moor.

Shakespeare, we may suppose, would not have inserted these lines in a later scene if he had wanted us to think that Iago's suspicions were invented on the spur of the moment to justify his villainy. Iago, however, is not so much concerned with Emilia's unfaithfulness, as with the fact that he is despised or pitied, or an object of ridicule as a cuckold; and this is intolerable to his self-esteem. The fact that this motive is not mentioned until this point does not in itself prove that it is merely a rationalization, for, of course, he would not mention it to Roderigo or to anyone else. It is considered respectable to act from feelings of injured merit: he could never admit that he feared he was an object of ridicule.

Booth was quite right to make Iago wince when Cassio kisses Emilia, for it leads on to the revelation in the second soliloquy that he fears Cassio with his night-cap too. His aside, spoken while Cassio is conversing with Desdemona, suggests that he is not merely pretending for his own ends that Cassio and Desdemona are in love with each other, but that he is, perhaps unconsciously, identifying himself with the supposedly amorous Cassio – 'Would they were clyster-pipes for your sake!' - and in the next soliloquy we learn why (II.1.282–98):

> Now, I do love her too;
> Not out of absolute lust – though peradventure
> I stand accountant for as great a sin –
> But partly led to diet my revenge
> For that I do suspect the lusty Moor
> Hath leaped into my seat, the thought whereof
> Doth, like a poisonous mineral, gnaw my inwards,
> And nothing can, or shall, content my soul
> Till I am evened with him, wife for wife;
> Or failing so, yet that I put the Moor

At least into a jealousy so strong
That judgement cannot cure. . . .
I'll have our Michael Cassio on the hip,
Abuse him to the Moor in the rank garb –
For I fear Cassio with my night-cap too. . . .

Here, if anywhere, is the motive-hunting of which Coleridge speaks. But, as Kittredge and others have argued,
Iago's jealousy is not a pretence but 'a raging torment'.
The image of the poisonous mineral convinces one by its
force and vividness. We may suspect that the professional
jealousy at Cassio's appointment only rankled so much
because Iago thought he had reason to hate Othello and
Cassio on other grounds.

We learn one other thing from these lines: that Iago
loves Desdemona, not, he tells us, 'out of absolute lust'
but partly to feed his revenge, either by cuckolding Othello
or getting someone else to do it for him. In Shakespeare's
source, as we have seen, the Ancient's love for Disdemona
is the primary motive for his actions. Shakespeare makes it
subordinate to others; but there are several hints earlier
in the play, and others on the first night in Cyprus, that
Iago is jealous of Othello's success with Desdemona, as
well as of his supposed seduction of Emilia. It is therefore
not surprising that in Act III, scene 3, Iago should be able
to describe the pangs of jealousy so vividly: he is drawing
on his own experience. He knows only too well

the green-eyed monster, which doth mock
The meat it feeds on

and he knows that

Dangerous conceits are in their natures poisons,
Which at the first are scarce found to distaste,
But, with a little act upon the blood,
Burn like the mines of sulphur.

19

The secret of Iago is not a motiveless malignity – though, being evil, he has a natural hatred of good – but a pathological jealousy of his wife, a suspicion of every man with whom she is acquainted, and a jealous love of Desdemona, which makes him take a vicarious pleasure in other men's actual or prospective enjoyment of her at the same time as it arouses his hatred of the successful Moor.

As Lily B. Campbell has shown, the Elizabethans recognized several different kinds of jealousy. Tofte in *The Blazon of Jealousie* (1613) described one sort, very like Iago's, as 'when we would not have that any one should obtain . . . that which we wish and desire to obtain'. Iago's jealousy is a kind of envy, which, Bacon tells us, is

> the vilest affection, and the most depraved; for which cause, it is the proper attribute of the Devil, who is called The Envious Man, that soweth tares amongst the wheat by night. *As it always cometh to pass, that Envy worketh subtilly, and in the dark; and to the prejudice of good things, such as is the wheat.*

Jealousy and envy are thus the springs of Iago's conduct, and his plot against Othello has the advantage of hurting the three people against whom he bears a grudge. Nor need we regard this multiplication of motives as incredible, for they all spring from the same basic attitude to life, the self-love of which he boasts to Roderigo, what Bacon called 'wisdom for a man's self'.

Iago has one more important soliloquy at the end of Act II, after he has suggested that Cassio should beg Desdemona to plead for him. Its main function is to explain to the audience why he has made this suggestion. But in the course of the speech he pays an indirect tribute to the depth of Othello's love for Desdemona; he admits that Desdemona is virtuous, despite his previous remarks about her, and that he is going to use her goodness to enmesh Othello and Cassio as well as her, and he speaks of the 'Divinity of hell' by which he is governed. His dedication to evil, revealed both here and in his first soliloquy, is as important to an understanding of his character as the psychological motives we have attempted to analyse. Othello is right to speak of him in the last scene as a demi-devil.

At the end of the play Iago is perfectly willing to confess what he has done, but he refuses to answer Othello's question (V.2.299):

> *Why he hath thus ensnared my soul and body?*

Some critics believe that he could not have answered the question, even if he had wanted to; but if the above analysis of his character has been sound, the reason for his obstinate silence is that he will reveal neither his own jealousy, nor his dedication to evil.

It is important to believe in the reality for him of Iago's motives. As with all Shakespeare's mature plays the dramatic relationship of one character to another is of great importance. It has often been pointed out that in *Hamlet* there are four young men who have the task of avenging their fathers – Laertes, Fortinbras and Pyrrhus, as well as Hamlet himself. So in *Othello* we observe the operations of jealousy in several different characters – in the comic dupe, Roderigo, in Bianca, in Iago and in Othello himself. The main theme is the way in which a jealous villain – whose villainy cannot be penetrated by anyone because of the impossibility of distinguishing between genuine and apparent honesty – succeeds in infecting an essentially noble man, one who is 'not easily jealous', with his own jealousy; and, in so doing, drags him down to his own level.

Those who have written on the imagery of the play have

shown how the hold Iago has over Othello is illustrated
by the language Shakespeare puts into their mouths. Both
characters use a great deal of animal imagery, and it is
interesting to note its distribution. Iago's occurs mostly in
the first three Acts of the play: he mentions, for example,
ass, daws, flies, ram, jennet, guinea-hen, baboon, wild-cat,
snipe, goats, monkeys, monster and wolves. Othello, on the
other hand, who makes no use of animal imagery in the
first two Acts of the play, catches the trick from Iago in
Acts III and IV. The fondness of both characters for
mentioning repulsive animals and insects is one way by
which Shakespeare shows the corruption of the Moor's
mind by his subordinate. Seven of Othello's animals had
been previously mentioned by Iago. Iago, for example, had
said (III.3.400) it would be impossible to catch Desdemona
and Cassio in the act of adultery,

> *Were they as prime as goats, as hot as monkeys.*

Later in the play, Othello, exasperated by Desdemona's
pleasure at Cassio's appointment as Governor of Cyprus,
exclaims 'Goats and monkeys!'

The same transference from Iago to Othello may be
observed in what S. L. Bethell called diabolic imagery.
He estimated that of the 64 images relating to hell and
damnation – many of them are allusions rather than strict
images – Iago has 18 and Othello 26. But 14 of Iago's are
used in the first two Acts, and 25 of Othello's in the last
three. The theme of hell originates with Iago and is trans-
ferred to Othello only when Iago has succeeded in infecting
the Moor with his jealousy.

If, then, this is the thematic structure of the play, it is
impossible to accept the view, which dates from Coleridge,
that jealousy was not the point of Othello's passion, or
Pushkin's remark, quoted by Dostoevsky in *The Brothers*

Karamazov, that 'Othello was not jealous, he was trustful'. We are told that in all the 78 productions of *Othello* in the Soviet Union between 1945 and 1957 only one actor interpreted the Moor as a man obsessed by jealousy. It is partly a matter of definition. Jealousy covers a wide variety of feelings from a crude sexual possessiveness to spiritual disillusionment, from groundless suspicion to a certain knowledge of marital unfaithfulness. Othello is not jealous in the same pathological way as Leontes, who needs no proof or prompter to make him certain that Hermione has played him false with his best friend. But, all the same, as Stoll pointed out, Othello does display the very characteristics of jealousy mentioned by Coleridge in his attempt to show that the Moor was not jealous: eagerness to snatch at proofs (for example, Cassio's dream, the handkerchief), a disposition to degrade the object of his passion by sensual fancies and images (for example, IV.1.35-43), catching occasions to ease the mind by ambiguities, a dread of vulgar ridicule, and a spirit of selfish vindictiveness (for example, 'I will chop her into messes'). This aspect of Othello cannot be ignored; but, at the same time, he is unable to stop loving the wife who, as he believes, has betrayed him. The love is partly sexual infatuation, but not merely that. In the scene in which he sees Bianca return the handkerchief to Cassio, Othello oscillates between ungovernable rage and pity for Desdemona's fall (IV.1.177-99):

> *A fine woman, a fair woman, a sweet woman! . . . Ay, let her rot and perish, and be damned tonight. . . She might lie by an emperor's side and command him tasks . . . so delicate with her needle, an admirable musician! . . . but yet the pity of it, Iago! O, Iago, the pity of it, Iago! . . . I will chop her into messes!*

The same ambivalence is to be seen in IV.2, where Othello treats Desdemona,

> *Who art so lovely fair, and smell'st so sweet*
> *That the sense aches at thee,*

as a whore; and in the last scene, where her snow-white skin and balmy breath

> *almost persuade*
> *Justice to break her sword.*

Mingled with his furious jealousy, and his fear of being despised as a cuckold, is the feeling that chaos is come again because he has garnered up his heart in Desdemona. His feelings are similar to those of Troilus when he witnesses Cressida's unfaithfulness:

> *The bonds of heaven are slipped, dissolved and loosed....*

But Othello is an older man than Troilus, and his dedication to love is more absolute because Desdemona was a worthier object than Cressida; and the corresponding disillusionment is more devastating. In Othello's case there is an additional complication. Like the jealous husbands in many French and Spanish plays of the seventeenth century and in plays by some Jacobean dramatists, Othello believes that his own honour is tarnished by his wife's unfaithfulness, and that he can only restore his honour by killing her and her paramour. It has been pointed out that this drama of marital honour is preceded in Act I by a drama of parental honour – Brabantio feels himself disgraced by his daughter's elopement – and in Act II by a drama of professional honour centred on Cassio, who feels he has lost the immortal part of himself in losing his reputation as a soldier.

Othello claims in his final apologia that he was 'not

easily jealous'; and some critics have regarded this statement as a delusion. Iago begins his temptation at line 35 of III.3, and some two hundred lines later Othello has become a prey to jealousy, when he says 'Set on thy wife to observe'. Until that point Othello has been worried by Iago's accusations, but he has not fallen. His comment on Iago's warning against jealousy 'O misery!' is not an admission that he has already fallen a victim. Even as late as line 223, when he says

> *I do not think but Desdemona's honest*

he is still not quite vanquished, though he has obviously been shaken by Iago's echo (line 204) of Brabantio's final warning (I.3.290):

> *She has deceived her father, and may thee. . .*

> *She did deceive her father, marrying you.*

The most poisonous shafts in Iago's armoury are the suggestion that Othello knows nothing about the real nature of sophisticated Venetian ladies and that Desdemona's choice of a Moor showed a perverted taste (III.3. 230–31) –

> *a will most rank,*
> *Foul disproportion, thoughts unnatural.*

But even after he has asked Iago to get Emilia to spy on Desdemona, as soon as he sees her he is reconverted to a belief in her fidelity (III.3.275–6):

> *If she be false, O, then heaven mocks itself!*
> *I'll not believe't.*

Those who suppose that Othello was easily jealous point to the fact that the scene we have been considering takes only ten or twelve minutes to perform. But, of course, the playing-time is not intended to correspond exactly to the time supposed to elapse in real life : inevitably there is some telescoping. Shakespeare, indeed, plays some strange tricks with time. Iago begins his temptation on the morning after the arrival in Cyprus. At the end of the scene he promises to murder Cassio within three days, and the impression we get from the remainder of the play is that the attempt on Cassio's life was made within the stipulated period. Certainly the action of the last two Acts of the play is more or less continuous and so is the section from the beginning of Act II to the end of Act III, scene 3. The only possible break occurs between the third and fourth scenes of Act III, and, although an interval of a week or more at this point would help to explain Bianca's complaint that Cassio had stayed away for a week, such an interval would conflict with the impression we get that events are moving very swiftly. From Iago's point of view, every hour increases the danger of his exposure. Shakespeare was faced with an acute problem. The action has to be exceedingly swift or it becomes incredible; and yet considerable time has to elapse or the action becomes incredible in another way. News of the dispersal of the Turkish fleet has to be conveyed to Venice and Lodovico has to travel to Cyprus with the appointment of Cassio as Governor. Shakespeare uses a double clock, as many critics have recognized; but no one will notice the discrepancies during an actual performance of the play.

There is one, more serious, difficulty. Iago accuses Desdemona of adultery on the day following the consummation of her marriage. As she travels to Cyprus on one boat and Cassio on another, there was no possible occasion between her elopement and her reunion with Othello when she could have committed adultery with Cassio. Shakespeare could have arranged for Desdemona and Cassio to travel to Cyprus on the same boat, or have allowed some time to elapse after the arrival in Cyprus before the brawl which leads to Cassio's dismissal. Presumably he avoided these solutions to his problem either because he did not wish to slow down the action, or because Iago's plot depends on Othello's comparative ignorance of his wife, or because he wished to deprive the Moor of all rational grounds for his jealousy.

In the crucial scene (III.3), Iago makes no attempt to provide even the flimsiest circumstantial evidence of Desdemona's guilt, until Othello is no longer in a fit state to think logically about it. He first exclaims 'I like not that' when Cassio hurries off to avoid meeting Othello. Then he picks up Desdemona's mention of the fact that Cassio had come a-wooing with Othello – either before his avowal of love or between the proposal and the elopement – warns Othello against jealousy, and then suggests that Desdemona is too friendly with Cassio. Up to this point, Iago can withdraw his imputations, protest that he has been misunderstood; and Othello can assume that Desdemona has been carrying on a more or less innocent flirtation with Cassio during his own wooing, and that their cordial friendship may lead to something less innocent. The seed of suspicion is planted, and Othello is left to himself.

Before Iago resumes the temptation he comes into possession of the handkerchief; but it is to be noticed that he does not use it at once. He waits to see how far Othello's mind has been poisoned. When by his talk of Desdemona's stolen hours of lust and by his demand for ocular proof of her adultery, Othello shows that he has gone much further in his imagination than Iago had done in his accusations, Iago produces his story of Cassio's dream. (If Othello were capable of rational thought at this point, he would know that Iago and Cassio had had no recent opportunity of sharing a bed.) Even after his account of the dream, Iago might still retreat. As he himself is careful to point out, it might be a true dream and yet prove only that Cassio was in love with Desdemona, not that he had seduced her, or that she was in love with him. But from Othello's reaction to the dream, Iago knows that he can safely mention the handkerchief. If he had mentioned it at first, Othello might have guessed that Desdemona had mislaid it, but now he is so blinded with passion that he can believe impossibilities. Cassio and Desdemona could not, during the action of the play, have committed 'the act of shame | A thousand times' as Othello asserts after the murder. Othello, as Iago had planned, has been put

> At least into a jealousy so strong
> That judgement cannot cure.

If one were to consider the play as an exact replica of real life, one would be worried not merely by Shakespeare's treatment of time, but also by some improbabilities in the action. The success of Iago's plot depends on the assumption that Othello would avoid a specific accusation of Desdemona until too late, that Emilia, in spite of her love for Desdemona, would not realize earlier the way in which Iago was using the handkerchief, and that Othello would not confront Cassio with Iago's accusations. From the point of view of naturalism, Iago has astonishing luck. But, of course, the conventions of poetic drama do not require this kind of verisimilitude; and we must never forget that Shakespeare wrote his plays to be performed, not to be read.

When Othello claims that he is 'not easily jealous' he means that it would never have entered his head to suspect Desdemona of infidelity but for Iago's plot. In spite of the

reputation of Moors in this respect, there is no doubt that
Shakespeare intended this claim to be true. Othello's final
speech, just before his suicide, is not a last example of his
lack of self-knowledge, but an objective statement, for the
audience as well as for the people on stage, of the tragedy.
Those critics who think that Othello was self-deluded and
self-dramatizing to the death are as mistaken as those who
suppose that his character is flawless. It is true, of course,
that if it had been flawless, Iago could not have succeeded;
but it is quite wrong to regard his nobility as hollow. The
testimony of all the main characters in the play is decisive.
Brabantio loved him; Lodovico speaks of him as 'the noble
Moor' 'once so good'; Cassio, who has good cause to hate
him, addresses him as 'Dear General' and speaks his
epitaph: 'he was great of heart'. The Duke declares that
he is more fair than black. Montano is delighted to hear
of Othello's appointment as Governor. But the most
significant testimony to Othello's character comes from
the one man who hates him. Iago confesses that the state
'Cannot with safety cast him' because 'Another of his
fathom they have none'. When he first outlines his plot
he declares (I.3.393–4):

> *The Moor is of a free and open nature,*
> *That thinks men honest that but seem to be so. . . .*

In a later soliloquy he is even more emphatic (II.1.279–80):

> *The Moor – howbeit that I endure him not –*
> *Is of a constant, loving, noble nature. . . .*

This testimony cannot be brushed aside as a corporate
delusion.

Nor, indeed, should Othello's sense of drama be regarded as a tendency to self-dramatization. His quiet
authority when he encounters Brabantio's servants (I.2.
59) –

Keep up your bright swords, for the dew will rust them

– his defence of his marriage before the senate, and the last speech which leads to his account of stabbing the 'malignant and . . . turbaned Turk' as a preparation for his own suicide, are examples of his sense of occasion, which is perfectly fitting in a great soldier of royal birth. Even his frequent expressions of self-esteem would be regarded by Shakespeare's audience, not as vanity, but as legitimate and proper pride. It was not then considered that a great man should pretend to be unconscious of his merits. Othello, after all, was perfectly justified in believing that his services to the state would out-tongue the complaints of Brabantio; he was right in believing that his royal birth and his merits made him worthy of Desdemona; and, as he put it in his final apologia (V.2.335):

> *I have done the state some service and they know't.*

Far from being a braggart soldier, Othello is modest in his claims.

It has nevertheless been argued by some critics that to the end of the play the Moor fails to realize the whole truth: that he blames the arts of the demi-devil, Iago, and fate, but does not recognize the extent of his own guilt. Such an interpretation is incompatible with the text of the last scene. Immediately after the murder, while he still believes in Desdemona's guilt, Othello regrets what he has done (lines 98–102):

> *I have no wife.*
> *O, insupportable! O heavy hour!*
> *Methinks it should be now a huge eclipse*
> *Of sun and moon, and that th'affrighted globe*
> *Should yawn at alteration.*

A few lines later, he tells Emilia:

> *It is the very error of the moon;*
> *She comes more nearer earth than she was wont,*
> *And makes men mad.*

The implication is that he has been driven mad. But when Desdemona tries to shield him by pretending she has committed suicide, Othello shows how horribly his reason has been darkened – or possibly, that the truth is beginning to dawn on it – by exclaiming (line 130):

> *She's like a liar gone to burning hell.*

A little later he admits:

> *O, I were damned beneath all depth in hell*
> *But that I did proceed upon just grounds. . . .*

When he learns that he has not proceeded on just grounds, he first attempts to avenge himself on Iago; but it is clear that he intends to kill himself. He asks 'why should honour outlive honesty?' Why should reputation outlive inner integrity? He admits that he has reached his journey's end.

It is true that he asks 'Who can control his fate?' and speaks of Desdemona as ill-starred, referring possibly to the derivation of her name, which means 'unfortunate'. But it is only Shakespeare's evil characters, such as Edmund in *King Lear*, who completely discount the influence of the stars; and Othello does not disclaim his responsibility for his actions. He recognizes that he is damned and he looks forward to an eternity of torture for his crime (lines 271–8):

> *When we shall meet at compt*
> *This look of thine will hurl my soul from heaven*

> *And fiends will snatch at it. . . .*
> >   *Whip me, ye devils,*
> *From the possession of this heavenly sight!*
> *Blow me about in winds! Roast me in sulphur!*
> *Wash me in steep-down gulfs of liquid fire!*

It is odd, in the light of these lines, that anyone should think that Othello is 'cheering himself up', or that he refuses to recognize his own guilt. In his final speech, after urging his hearers to extenuate nothing, nor to set down aught in malice, he stabs himself as he had once in Aleppo stabbed a traducer of the state.

We have seen how Cinthio's Moor lives happily in Venice with his bride for some unspecified time. Shakespeare eliminated this period of happiness because if Othello were to have had this experience of peaceful marriage he would not have believed Iago's insinuations against Desdemona. The consummation of his marriage has to be postponed by the exigencies of war; and the first night in Cyprus is disturbed by the brawl which leads to the dismissal of Cassio. Iago begins his temptation on the following morning, and he is able to exploit Othello's comparative ignorance of his wife.

This ignorance is only partly due to the fact that they have had no opportunity of living together. It is due to a number of other factors. Othello comes of royal birth but he has won for himself a place of distinction in the service of the Venetian state by his military prowess. He confesses the one-sidedness of his experience (I.3.86–7):

> *little of this great world can I speak*
> *More than pertains to feats of broil and battle. . . .*

From the age of seven he has lived in the camp. He is very conscious of his lack of sophistication; and, although he is a natural orator, he thinks of himself as rude in his speech, and as being ignorant of the arts of polite conversation. He is a Christian, but we are conscious that he has not entirely outgrown some pagan superstitions. Brabantio 'loves' him, but it does not enter his head that the Moor is a possible son-in-law, because of the difference of race. Desdemona falls in love with his autobiography rather than with him. She loves him for the dangers he has undergone, partly because she pities past sufferings, partly because she wishes she could have had such exciting adventures herself – she is not called 'fair warrior' for nothing – and partly because she responded to the nobility, the integrity, and the simplicity of the great soldier. She 'saw Othello's visage in his mind' and this made the difference of colour seem irrelevant. But though her instinct about Othello was sound, she was acting on faith rather than knowledge.

But the difference of race and colour remains: the very feeling of 'otherness', which can be a recurrent miracle in marriage, can also be the seed from which distrust will spring. In a marriage of two different races this 'otherness' can be distorted and warped into alienation. The strangeness can come to seem a mask, hiding the real self. The act of faith and commitment can be interpreted as a perversion, as it was by Iago; but Shakespeare actually proves the essential innocence of the marriage by raising and quashing the suspicions an audience was bound to have.

Apart from the major difference of race between the couple, there is a great difference of age. Othello has reached middle age, apparently without any previous experience of love. At least he knows nothing about the manners and morals of Venetian ladies which, to judge not merely from Iago's satire but from Emilia's conversation and Roderigo's ambitions, leave something to be desired. In one respect Othello is lacking in self-knowledge.

He believes that he has reached an age in which the violent passions of youth have died down, so that his affections are guided by reason. He speaks scornfully of 'light-winged toys | Of feathered Cupid'; he is confident that love will never interfere with his duties as a soldier; and he claims (I.3.258–62) that he wishes Desdemona to accompany him to Cyprus not primarily 'To please the palate of [his] appetite',

> *But to be free and bounteous to her mind.*

What he does not fully realize at first is the absoluteness of his commitment to his love, and his dependence on her love for him. If he ceased to love her, chaos would come again; if he ceased to love her, his whole life would be drained of meaning and, full as it had been before he met her, his occupation would be gone. Equally important is his failure to know his own capacity for jealousy – that, though 'not easily jealous', he could be wrought by spurious evidence and become perplexed in the extreme.

Because of his lack of experience of women and because he has no reason to suspect Iago's integrity or to know of his hidden hatred for himself, he trusts his comrade-in-arms instead of the bride, who is still a comparative stranger. As Chapman remarked of a hero who has something in common with Othello:

> *He would believe, since he would be believed:*
> *Your noblest natures are most credulous.*

Edgar in *King Lear* is another character to whom these words could be applied; and it must be remembered that Othello's credulity with regard to Iago is shared by nearly all the characters in the play, even if Shakespeare was relying partly on the convention, common in Elizabethan drama, of 'the calumniator believed'.

34

Johnson gave as one of the proofs of Shakespeare's knowledge of human nature 'the fiery openness of Othello, magnanimous, artless, and credulous, boundless in his confidence, ardent in his affection, inflexible in his resolution and obdurate in his revenge'. This is a fair summary of the character of the Moor. It properly avoids the two extremes of interpretation – the assumption that he is faultless and the assumption that his nobility is hollow, which, as we have seen, is disproved even by Iago who is desperately anxious to believe the worst about human nature, and to drag everyone down to his own level. Love is merely lust, a proper pride is bragging, nobility is ostentation, and honesty a cloak for hypocrisy. To look at the play through the eyes of the villain is bound to give one a false impression. What Iago does is to exploit the virtues as well as the weaknesses of the Moor and of Desdemona, weaknesses both of character and situation. The noble simplicity of Othello,

> *Whose nature is so far from doing harm*
> *That he suspects none,*

and the warmth of Desdemona in championing Cassio's cause are the two qualities which provide Iago with his opportunity; but he would not have succeeded without the defects in the two characters. Desdemona's advocacy of Cassio is an interference in professional matters, and she is prepared to carry it almost to the extent of nagging. Equally serious, perhaps, is the fib she tells about the handkerchief, though we can excuse this by the fact that she is shocked and frightened by Othello's first outburst of fury. Othello's weaknesses are also vulnerable. His freedom from suspicion which is based on his own transparent sincerity leads to an absurd credulity and it reveals an ignorance of human nature. His pride in his own

35

achievements and his sense of honour are linked with the common delusion that a man's honour can be smirched by his wife's misbehaviour and redeemed only by her death. Above all, he is too confident of his own rationality and of the way his passions are under his control.

Iago makes use of these weaknesses of character, but he seizes too on the peculiarities of the marriage – the fact that it involved deception of Brabantio; the difference of race which could be represented as being an unnatural basis for marriage between 'an erring barbarian and a super-subtle Venetian', which would collapse as soon as she was sated with his body; the difference of age, which could be used to plant doubts in Othello's mind about his competence as a lover compared with a younger man; and the separation of the couple on the day of their secret marriage. Add to this the fact that Iago is not merely cunning but lucky: he obtains possession of the handkerchief at the very moment when he needs some circumstantial evidence, and Bianca accosts Cassio with the handkerchief in Othello's sight so that Iago can turn the incident to his advantage.

Iago ruins himself in the end because of his degraded view of human nature. He was afraid that Roderigo would demand the return of his presents, because he knew that men were animated by self-interest; he was afraid that Othello would have it out with Cassio; but he was too obtuse to realize that his wife, because of her love for Desdemona, would court death rather than let her memory be smirched. But, before his exposure, Iago has succeeded in his aim of driving Othello 'into a jealousy so strong | That judgement cannot cure' and of destroying both the Moor and his wife, although this was not his original intention.

In the course of the play we watch the gradual destruc-

tion of Othello's integrity, and the nobler we take him to
be in the first Act the more painful is the spectacle. Little
by little we see the devout Christian revert to barbarism,
the great soldier reduced to being a powerless puppet, the
man of noble self-control driven into unreasoning frenzy,
the chivalric lover striking his wife in public, the devoted
husband murdering the woman he still loves. In *Twelfth
Night*, Orsino, when he believes that Olivia has married
Cesario, asks her why he should not

> *Kill what I love – a savage jealousy*
> *That sometime savours nobly?*

Othello kills what he loves, because he believes in his state
of darkened reason that this is the only way to restore his
lost honour (V.2.1–2):

> *It is the cause, it is the cause, my soul:*
> *Let me not name it to you, you chaste stars!*

In this last scene Othello has recovered something of his
dignity and self-control. But he is still deluded. He thinks
that the murder he is committing is a sacrifice to his ideal
of love; that what he is doing is an act of justice, not of
revenge for his wounded self-esteem; that he is doing it
lest she 'betray more men'. Some memory of the Christian
ethic he is violating makes him offer Desdemona a chance
of making her peace with God; but the actual murder is
committed in a rage, when Desdemona weeps for Cassio.
His savage jealousy does not savour nobly; but when,
after the murder, he learns how he has been deluded and
what he has lost, he recovers his former nobility, his
greatness of heart.

In speaking his own epitaph, Othello claims that he had
'loved not wisely, but too well'. This is true. If he had
loved less intensely, if he had not garnered up his heart in

Desdemona, if she had not been the fountain from which
his current ran, his reaction to her supposed unfaithfulness
would not have been so violent, or so disastrous. He re-
tains some sympathy, even in his most horrible behaviour,
because we remember his earlier nobility, reflected in the
poetry, because we are conscious all the time that he has
become Iago's puppet, because we are aware of the struggle
in his mind between love and perverted views of 'honour',
and because he is not merely sexually jealous and 'Perplexed in the extreme', but also suffering from a profound
spiritual disillusionment. Coleridge, as we have seen, was
wrong in supposing that jealousy was not the point in
Othello's passion, but he was right in seeing that it was also

> an agony that the creature, whom he had believed an-
> gelic . . . whom he could not help still loving, should be
> proved impure and worthless . . . It was a moral indignation
> that virtue should so fall.

Critics, on the whole, have looked on *Othello* as inferior
to *King Lear* and *Macbeth*, the tragedies which immediately
followed it; but it was 'preeminently dear' to Wordsworth;
and Landor, in answering the criticism that Shakespeare
was less grand in his designs than other poets, replied:

> To the eye. But Othello was loftier than the citadel of
> Troy; and what a Paradise fell before him! Let us descend;
> for from Othello we must descend, whatever road we take.

Landor implies that the play is the equal of the *Iliad* and
Paradise Lost in the magnitude of its theme. But most
critics today would regard such praise as excessive; partly
because they feel that the play depends too much on
theatrical convention – a gullible hero deceived by a melodramatic villain – and also on codes of behaviour which
can no longer be regarded as valid. *Hamlet* is not damaged

for us by the fact that we no longer believe in the revenge code, which its hero in fact transcends, and the mythological impression given by *King Lear* prevents us from expecting verisimilitude. *Othello* is Shakespeare's only domestic tragedy, and the only one which is set in his own age; and we are likely to be more disturbed by the operations of poetic licence. We may also be inclined to feel that it lacks the universality and cosmic overtones of the other great tragedies. If, however, the interpretation offered above is sound, *Othello* is clearly not without universal significance, for, apart from its dramatization of the difficulty of discovering reality behind appearance, its two main characters exemplify opposing principles which together constitute the human psyche. Othello believes in love, in complete commitment, in nobility, in vocation, and in absolutes. Iago believes in nothing, and least of all in other human beings. Love to him is merely sex, 'a lust of the blood and a permission of the will'. He is unable to love, as can be seen from the fact that his professed love for Desdemona is merely a means to an end – of revenging himself on Othello: love is an instrument of hate. Virtue to him is an illusion or an absurdity, Desdemona's admitted goodness being an opportunity for exploitation. The sensible man is governed entirely by self-interest. The good are simpletons who can be led by the nose; other people, good or bad, are objects to be manipulated. Iago is the Italianate villain raised to the highest pitch of intensity; he is what the Elizabethans called a malcontent; he is the intellect divorced from the imagination; he is the corrosive which eats away love and trust; 'he publishes doubt and calls it knowledge' (in Blake's phrase); he is the spirit that denies; he is Shakespeare's most penetrating vision of evil, beside which Edmund in *King Lear* seems almost amiable.

Keats remarked that Shakespeare took as much delight

39

in conceiving an Iago as an Imogen. We may go further and suggest that he knew the psychology of Iago from the inside. It has often been observed that Iago, like Shakespeare himself, was an actor; and Bradley pointed out that, in formulating his plots, Iago resembles a dramatist in the early stages of composition. It may be added that a dramatist manipulates his characters, as Iago manipulated other people. This does not mean, of course, that Shakespeare had a similar dedication to evil; but, the greater the dramatist, the greater his capacity to imagine himself in all kinds of characters. Thersites is as convincing as Troilus; and though, as we can see from the *Sonnets*, Shakespeare affirmed his faith in love, there must have been occasions when the vision of Iago seemed more rational. However much we are appalled by Iago's actions, most of us are occasionally tempted to see things from his point of view. In a sense, therefore, the conflict between Othello and Iago is one which has a much wider application than the particular circumstances of the play.

We have concentrated attention on the two principal characters, on whom any interpretation of the play mainly depends and about whom there is most critical debate, and commented only incidentally on the remaining characters. A few words may be added on these.

Some modern critics have spoken harshly of Desdemona. They have stressed her deceit of her father, her unwise intervention on behalf of Cassio, and her lie to Othello about the loss of the handkerchief: they have even blamed her last words in which she mendaciously exonerates her murderer. But those who speak of the 'guilt' of Desdemona are surely as far from the truth as those who regard her as a female Christ-figure. For her essential goodness, in which she 'Does tire the ingener', is vouched for both by her

actions and by the testimony of the other characters.
Brabantio, in accusing Othello, stresses his daughter's
innocence; Iago finds it difficult to persuade Roderigo that
she is not full of 'most blessed condition'; Cassio's chaste
admiration is apparent throughout the play; he describes
her hyperbolically as 'a maid | That paragons description'
and politely but firmly repudiates Iago's lascivious imputations; the worldly-wise and cynical Emilia is inspired
by her love for her mistress to die in defence of her memory;
and even Iago, in framing his plot against the Moor, admits
that he is going to use Desdemona's 'goodness' as a net to
enmesh both Othello and Cassio. Othello refers to her, and
she refers to herself, as a warrior; she falls in love with
Othello because of his adventures, which she envies; the
extraordinary abnegation and selflessness of her character
are revealed in her reactions to Othello's jealousy and in
her last sublime falsehood. What faults of judgement she
displays are all due to her youth and inexperience.

Cassio is defined partly by the exigencies of the plot,
which require him to have a poor head for drinking and to
have a mistress; but his chivalric worship of Desdemona,
his affectionate admiration for Othello, which enables him
even at the end to call him 'Dear General' and to speak of
his greatness of heart, and his professional reputation,
which only Iago impugns, build up a complex portrait of
an attractive, if flawed, character. In spite of his weaknesses, we can understand why Iago should be envious of
the 'daily beauty in his life' and why Desdemona should
speak so warmly for his reinstatement.

Emilia's character, too, is determined by the plot. In the
source, the villain's wife is privy to his nefarious designs.
Shakespeare wisely makes her, like the other characters,
ignorant of Iago's character. She knows that she has lost
his love, and her unhappy marriage drives her to cynicism

about sex; but she tries to win back her husband's affections by carrying out his wishes, even when this involves
betrayal of the mistress she loves. If we examine her role
too curiously, we may be inclined to think her dull-witted
not to realize the truth before the last scene; and her
superb defiance of Othello and Iago may appear to be
inconsistent with the worldly standards she has previously
enunciated. But, during a performance, her failure to
penetrate Iago's hypocrisy appears to be an additional
proof of its impenetrability, rather than of her stupidity;
and her cynical talk is not ultimately incompatible with
heroic action.

Roderigo, 'God Almighty's fool', begins as a gulled
gentleman, honestly, if sentimentally, in love with Desdemona; and he ends as a would-be adulterer and a potential
murderer, his feeble jealousy a parody of Othello's. We see
him only in relation to his evil genius, Iago, whose powers
of corruption he afterwards exercises on a nobler victim.
The scenes in which he appears provide the only sub-
stantial comic relief; the Clown himself hardly raises a
smile, and Cassio's intoxication, amusing in itself, is over-
shadowed by our consciousness of Iago's design against
him.

The other characters – Brabantio, Montano, Gratiano,
Lodovico – are merely sketched; but, within the limits
of their presentation, they are perfectly adequate for Shakespeare's purpose.

Lastly, a word should be said about the poetry of the
play. We have touched on the question of imagery in relation to the corruption of Othello by Iago. It has often
been pointed out that the characters are differentiated by
the imagery they use. Both Othello and Iago, for example,
use sea imagery, but in a totally different way; the one

romantic, as in the famous description of the Black Sea flowing through the Sea of Marmora into the Dardanelles, and the other prosaic. There is a similar difference in the characters' references to their own profession: to Othello it is a vocation, to Iago it is a trade. Both characters, again, use images of wealth. Iago, characteristically, speaks of actual money; Othello talks rather of the chrysolite and the pearl. It has been pointed out, too, that while Othello's characteristic image is the metaphor, Iago's is the simile; and this fits in with the villain's conscious manipulation of all the people with whom he comes in contact.

Several other groups of images (which have been examined in some detail by R. B. Heilman) may be mentioned. The theme of witchcraft, first introduced by Brabantio to account for the unnaturalness of his daughter's marriage, is taken up by Iago in the temptation scene, and finds its most memorable expression in Othello's account of the handkerchief. The fact that the handkerchief was not merely a love-token and the Moor's first gift to Desdemona, but that it was thought also to have magical properties, goes far to explain why he should be 'Perplexed in the extreme' by its loss. It also shows, perhaps, that pagan superstitions have not been entirely eradicated by the Moor's baptism; and Desdemona's half-belief in the magic deters her from admitting that the handkerchief is lost.

The theme of light and darkness is more complex. It begins with the simple contrast between the complexions of Desdemona and Othello; it quickly takes on a moral connotation with the devilish blackness of the Moor covering a noble soul; and, later in the play, to his diseased imagination, the whiteness of Desdemona seems to hide the blackness of sin. In the last scene, Othello is described as a 'blacker devil' for murdering the angelic Desdemona.

A minor example of image-patterns is connected with drugs and poisons. It ranges from the drug which Braban-tio accuses Othello of using in order to subdue Desde-mona's affections, to the coloquintida to which Iago hopes to reduce the sweetness of Othello's love, the poison of jealousy he administers to his victim, the mandragora which will fail to bring him rest, and the poisonous mineral to which Iago compares his own jealousy.

The imagery is only one form of figurative expression; and the total effect of what Wilson Knight has called 'the Othello music' in creating our imaginative impression of the hero depends on a wide range of poetic devices, in-cluding exotic colouring and the actual sound of the verse. As some recent critics have professed to find something hollow in Othello's nobility and have argued that this is revealed by the poetic rhetoric, it may be necessary to affirm that the diction, the imagery and the music of Othello's speech cannot properly be used to undermine his nobility. To most sensitive critics his lines ring true.

FURTHER READING

Editions with fuller commentary than the present one
allows include the Arden (edited by M. R. Ridley, 1958),
the Cambridge (edited by Alice Walker and J. Dover
Wilson, 1957), and the New Cambridge (edited by Norman
Sanders, 1984). (See An Account of the Text, p. 219.) The
best-known interpretation of the play is given in A. C.
Bradley's *Shakespearean Tragedy* (1904). This has been
attacked by numerous critics: E. E. Stoll, as early as 1915
and in *Art and Artifice in Shakespeare* (1933), claimed that
the character of the hero was psychologically inconsistent;
in 'Diabolic Intellect and the Noble Hero', F. R. Leavis
argued that Bradley had sentimentalized the character. The
article was reprinted in *The Common Pursuit* (1952;
Peregrine Books 1962). Stoll was answered effectively by
J. I. M. Stewart in *Character and Motive in Shakespeare*
(1949), and there have been refutations of Leavis by Helen
Gardner in *The Noble Moor* (1956), in John Bayley's *The
Characters of Love* (1960), and in John Holloway's *The
Story of the Night* (1962). There is a famous essay on the
play in *The Wheel of Fire* by G. Wilson Knight (1930).
Shakespeare Survey 21 (1968) contains nine articles on the
play. Most of these, including Gardner's survey of modern
criticism, were reprinted in *Aspects of Othello*, edited by
Kenneth Muir and Philip Edwards (1977).

The fullest account of the imagery of the play is to be
found in *Magic in the Web* by R. B. Heilman (1956). There
are articles by M. M. Morozov and S. L. Bethell (both
reprinted in *Aspects*), a chapter in *The Development of
Shakespeare's Imagery* by W. H. Clemen (1951), and an
essay on the iteration of 'honest' in William Empson's *The
Structure of Complex Words* (1951).

There is a detailed account of the action of the play in Granville Barker's *Preface* (1930) and a comprehensive commentary in Martin Elliott's *Shakespeare's Invention of Othello* (1988). Marvin Rosenberg in *The Masks of Othello* (1961) deals with the interaction of stage performance and literary interpretation. *Stanislavsky Produces Othello* (by Stanislavsky himself, 1948) and Arthur Colby Sprague's *Shakespearean Players and Performances* (1954) are invaluable. So, too, is G. K. Hunter's lecture 'Othello and Colour Prejudice' (reprinted in *Dramatic Identities and Cultural Tradition* (1978)).

There is a valuable chapter on the play by Robert Hapgood in *Shakespeare: Select Biographical Guides*, edited by Stanley Wells (1973; new edition 1990). There is an interesting book on *Iago* by Stanley Edgar Hyman (1970), and an excellent article by Giorgio Melchiori on Shakespeare's use of rhetoric in *Othello* in *Shakespeare Survey 34* (1981). A chapter in *Shakespeare's Tragic Sequence* (1979) gives Kenneth Muir's more recent views on the play.

The main source is included in *Elizabethan Love Stories*, edited by T. J. B. Spencer (Penguin Shakespeare Library, 1968). Shakespeare's treatment of his various sources is discussed by Kenneth Muir in *The Sources of Shakespeare's Plays* (1977) and more extensively by Geoffrey Bullough in *Narrative and Dramatic Sources of Shakespeare, VIII* (1973). He prints the main source, together with a Bandello story translated by Geoffrey Fenton (1567) and an extract from *The Generall Historie of the Turkes* (1603) by Richard Knolles.

OTHELLO

THE CHARACTERS IN THE PLAY

OTHELLO, a Moor, General in the Venetian army
DESDEMONA, his wife
CASSIO, his Lieutenant
IAGO, his Ancient
EMILIA, wife of Iago
BIANCA, mistress of Cassio
RODERIGO, in love with Desdemona

THE DUKE OF VENICE
BRABANTIO, a Venetian Senator, Desdemona's father
GRATIANO, his brother
LODOVICO, his kinsman
MONTANO, Governor of Cyprus

Senators of Venice
Gentlemen of Cyprus
Musicians
Officers
A Clown in Othello's household
A Herald
A Sailor
A Messenger
Soldiers, attendants, and servants

Enter Roderigo and Iago   I.1

RODERIGO

   Tush, never tell me! I take it much unkindly

   That thou, Iago, who hast had my purse

   As if the strings were thine, shouldst know of this.

IAGO

   'Sblood, but you will not hear me!

   If ever I did dream of such a matter,

   Abhor me.

RODERIGO

   Thou told'st me thou didst hold him in thy hate.

IAGO

   Despise me, if I do not. Three great ones of the city,

   In personal suit to make me his Lieutenant,

   Off-capped to him: and by the faith of man,   10

   I know my price, I am worth no worse a place.

   But he, as loving his own pride and purposes,

   Evades them with a bombast circumstance   *ignores*

   Horribly stuffed with epithets of war,   *mediators*

   And in conclusion

   Non-suits my mediators. For 'Certes,' says he,

   'I have already chose my officer.'

   And what was he?

   Forsooth, a great arithmetician,

   One Michael Cassio, a Florentine –   20

   A fellow almost damned in a fair wife –   *thought to be*

   That never set a squadron in the field,   *an inevitable*

   Nor the division of a battle knows   *target for being*

                    51   *cuckolded*   ~~seduction~~ –
                                           dramatic irony

More than a spinster - unless the bookish theoric,
Wherein the togèd consuls can propose
As masterly as he. Mere prattle without practice
Is all his soldiership. But he, sir, had th'election:
And I, of whom his eyes had seen the proof
At Rhodes, at Cyprus, and on other grounds

30   Christian and heathen, must be leed and calmed
By debitor and creditor; this counter-caster,
He in good time must his Lieutenant be,
And I - God bless the mark! - his Moorship's Ancient.

RODERIGO

By heaven, I rather would have been his hangman.

IAGO

Why, there's no remedy. 'Tis the curse of service:
Preferment goes by letter and affection,
And not by old gradation, where each second
Stood heir to th'first. Now sir, be judge yourself
Whether I in any just term am affined

40   To love the Moor.

RODERIGO

I would not follow him then.

IAGO   O, sir, content you:

I follow him to serve my turn upon him.
We cannot all be masters, nor all masters
Cannot be truly followed. You shall mark
Many a duteous and knee-crooking knave
That, doting on his own obsequious bondage,
Wears out his time, much like his master's ass,
For naught but provender, and when he's old -
        cashiered!
Whip me such honest knaves. Others there are

50   Who, trimmed in forms and visages of duty,
Keep yet their hearts attending on themselves,
And, throwing but shows of service on their lords,

Do well thrive by them; and when they have lined their
      coats,
Do themselves homage: these fellows have some soul,
And such a one do I profess myself.
For, sir,
It is as sure as you are Roderigo,
Were I the Moor, I would not be Iago:
In following him, I follow but myself.
Heaven is my judge, not I for love and duty,   60
But seeming so for my peculiar end:
For when my outward action doth demonstrate
The native act and figure of my heart
In compliment extern, 'tis not long after,
But I will wear my heart upon my sleeve
For daws to peck at — I am not what I am.

RODERIGO

What a full fortune does the thick-lips owe
If he can carry't thus!

IAGO   Call up her father,
Rouse him, make after him, poison his delight,
Proclaim him in the streets; incense her kinsmen,   70
And, though he in a fertile climate dwell,
Plague him with flies: though that his joy be joy,
Yet throw such chances of vexation on't,
As it may lose some colour.

RODERIGO

Here is her father's house; I'll call aloud.

IAGO

Do, with like timorous accent and dire yell,
As when, by night and negligence, the fire
Is spied in populous cities.

RODERIGO

What, ho, Brabantio! Signor Brabantio, ho!

I.1

IAGO

80   Awake! What, ho, Brabantio! Thieves, thieves!
      Look to your house, your daughter, and your bags!
      Thieves, thieves!
            Enter Brabantio above, at a window

BRABANTIO
      What is the reason of this terrible summons?
      What is the matter there?

RODERIGO
      Signor, is all your family within?

IAGO
      Are your doors locked?

BRABANTIO   Why, wherefore ask you this?

IAGO
      Zounds, sir, you're robbed; for shame, put on your
            gown;
      Your heart is burst, you have lost half your soul.
      Even now, now, very now, an old black ram
90   Is tupping your white ewe. Arise, arise,
      Awake the snorting citizens with the bell,
      Or else the devil will make a grandsire of you.
      Arise, I say!

BRABANTIO   What, have you lost your wits?

RODERIGO
      Most reverend signor, do you know my voice?

BRABANTIO
      Not I: what are you?

RODERIGO   My name is Roderigo.

BRABANTIO
      The worser welcome!
      I have charged thee not to haunt about my doors.
      In honest plainness thou hast heard me say
      My daughter is not for thee. And now in madness,
100   Being full of supper and distempering draughts,

54

Upon malicious bravery dost thou come
To start my quiet.

RODERIGO
  Sir, sir, sir –

BRABANTIO   But thou must needs be sure
  My spirit and my place have in them power
  To make this bitter to thee.

RODERIGO   Patience, good sir.

BRABANTIO
  What tell'st thou me of robbing? This is Venice:
  My house is not a grange. *house in the country*

RODERIGO   Most grave Brabantio,
  In simple and pure soul I come to you . . .

IAGO Zounds, sir, you are one of those that will not serve
  God if the devil bid you. Because we come to do you 110
  service, and you think we are ruffians, you'll have your
  daughter covered with a Barbary horse; you'll have your
  nephews neigh to you, you'll have coursers for cousins,
  and jennets for germans. *animal imagery note*

BRABANTIO What profane wretch art thou?

IAGO I am one, sir, that comes to tell you, your daughter
  and the Moor are now making the beast with two
  backs.

BRABANTIO
  Thou art a villain.

IAGO   You are a Senator.

BRABANTIO
  This thou shalt answer. I know thee, Roderigo.   120

RODERIGO
  Sir, I will answer anything. But I beseech you
  If't be your pleasure and most wise consent,
  As partly I find it is, that your fair daughter,
  At this odd-even and dull watch o'th'night,
  Transported with no worse nor better guard

But with a knave of common hire, a gondolier,
To the gross clasps of a lascivious Moor –
If this be known to you, and your allowance,
We then have done you bold and saucy wrongs;
130 But if you know not this, my manners tell me
We have your wrong rebuke. Do not believe
That from the sense of all civility
I thus would play and trifle with your reverence.
Your daughter, if you have not given her leave,
I say again hath made a gross revolt,
Tying her duty, beauty, wit, and fortunes
In an extravagant and wheeling stranger
Of here and everywhere. Straight satisfy yourself:
If she be in her chamber or your house,
140 Let loose on me the justice of the state
For thus deluding you.

BRABANTIO   Strike on the tinder, ho!
Give me a taper; call up all my people!
This accident is not unlike my dream:
Belief of it oppresses me already.
Light, I say, light!   *Exit above*

IAGO   Farewell, for I must leave you.
It seems not meet, nor wholesome to my place,
To be produced – as if I stay, I shall –
Against the Moor. For I do know the state,
However this may gall him with some check,
150 Cannot with safety cast him; for he's embarked
With such loud reason to the Cyprus wars,
Which even now stand in act, that for their souls
Another of his fathom they have none
To lead their business. In which regard,
Though I do hate him as I do hell pains,
Yet for necessity of present life
I must show out a flag and sign of love,

Which is indeed but sign. That you shall surely find him,
Lead to the Sagittary the raisèd search;
And there will I be with him. So farewell.   *Exit* 160
    Enter Brabantio in his night-gown with servants and
    torches

BRABANTIO
  It is too true an evil. Gone she is,
  And what's to come of my despisèd time
  Is naught but bitterness. Now, Roderigo,
  Where didst thou see her? – O unhappy girl! –
  With the Moor, say'st thou? – Who would be a father? –
  How didst thou know 'twas she? – O, she deceives me
  Past thought! – What said she to you? – Get more tapers.
  Raise all my kindred. – Are they married, think you?

RODERIGO
  Truly I think they are.

BRABANTIO
  O heaven! How got she out? O treason of the blood!   170
  Fathers, from hence trust not your daughters' minds
  By what you see them act. Is there not charms
  By which the property of youth and maidhood
  May be abused? Have you not read, Roderigo,
  Of some such thing?

RODERIGO   Yes, sir, I have indeed.

BRABANTIO
  Call up my brother – O would you had had her!
  Some one way, some another. Do you know
  Where we may apprehend her and the Moor?

RODERIGO
  I think I can discover him, if you please
  To get good guard and go along with me.   180

BRABANTIO
  Pray you, lead on. At every house I'll call –
  I may command at most. Get weapons, ho!

> And raise some special officers of night.
> On, good Roderigo, I'll deserve your pains.   *Exeunt*

I.2   *Enter Othello, Iago, attendants with torches*
IAGO
> Though in the trade of war I have slain men,
> Yet do I hold it very stuff o'th'conscience
> To do no contrived murder: I lack iniquity
> Sometimes to do me service. Nine or ten times
> I had thought t'have yerked him here under the ribs.
OTHELLO
> 'Tis better as it is.
IAGO   Nay, but he prated
> And spoke such scurvy and provoking terms
> Against your honour,
> That with the little godliness I have,
10 I did full hard forbear him. But I pray, sir,
> Are you fast married? For be assured of this,
> That the Magnifico is much beloved,
> And hath in his effect a voice potential
> As double as the Duke's. He will divorce you,
> Or put upon you what restraint and grievance
> That law, with all his might to enforce it on,
> Will give him cable.
OTHELLO   Let him do his spite:
> My services, which I have done the signory,
> Shall out-tongue his complaints. 'Tis yet to know –
20 Which, when I know that boasting is an honour,
> I shall provulgate – I fetch my life and being
> From men of royal siege, and my demerits
> May speak, unbonneted, to as proud a fortune
> As this that I have reached. For know, Iago,
> But that I love the gentle Desdemona,

58

I would not my unhousèd free condition
Put into circumscription and confine
For the seas' worth. But look, what lights come yond!

IAGO

Those are the raisèd father and his friends:
You were best go in.

OTHELLO   Not I: I must be found.   30
My parts, my title, and my perfect soul
Shall manifest me rightly. Is it they?

IAGO

By Janus, I think no. God of entrance. facing both ways

Enter Cassio, with men bearing torches

OTHELLO

The servants of the Duke and my Lieutenant!
The goodness of the night upon you, friends.
What is the news?

CASSIO   The Duke does greet you, General,
And he requires your haste-post-haste appearance
Even on the instant.

OTHELLO   What is the matter, think you?

CASSIO

Something from Cyprus, as I may divine:
It is a business of some heat. The galleys   40
Have sent a dozen sequent messengers
This very night at one another's heels;
And many of the consuls, raised and met,
Are at the Duke's already. You have been hotly called
          for,
When being not at your lodging to be found.
The senate hath sent about three several quests
To search you out.

OTHELLO   'Tis well I am found by you:
I will but spend a word here in the house
And go with you.   *Exit*

I.2

CASSIO   Ancient, what makes he here?

IAGO

50   Faith, he tonight hath boarded a land carack:
      If it prove lawful prize, he's made for ever.

CASSIO

      I do not understand.

IAGO   He's married.

CASSIO   To who?

IAGO

      Marry, to – Come, Captain, will you go?
          Enter Othello

OTHELLO   Have with you.

CASSIO

      Here comes another troop to seek for you.
          Enter Brabantio, Roderigo, with officers and torches

IAGO

      It is Brabantio: General, be advised,
      He comes to bad intent.

oily

OTHELLO   Holla, stand there.

RODERIGO

      Signor, it is the Moor.

BRABANTIO   Down with him, thief!

IAGO

      You, Roderigo? Come, sir, I am for you.   *to Othello*

OTHELLO

      Keep up your bright swords, for the dew will rust them.
60   Good signor, you shall more command with years
      Than with your weapons.

Dignity & courtesy

BRABANTIO

      O thou foul thief! Where hast thou stowed my daughter?
      Damned as thou art, thou hast enchanted her:
      For I'll refer me to all things of sense,
      If she in chains of magic were not bound,
      Whether a maid, so tender, fair, and happy,

60

So opposite to marriage that she shunned
The wealthy curlèd darlings of our nation,
Would ever have – t'incur a general mock –
Run from her guardage to the sooty bosom   70
Of such a thing as thou: to fear, not to delight.
Judge me the world, if 'tis not gross in sense
That thou hast practised on her with foul charms,
Abused her delicate youth with drugs or minerals
That weakens motion. I'll have't disputed on; *go to law.*
'Tis probable, and palpable to thinking:
I therefore apprehend, and do attach thee
For an abuser of the world, a practiser
Of arts inhibited, and out of warrant.
Lay hold upon him: if he do resist,   80
Subdue him, at his peril.

OTHELLO   Hold your hands,
Both you of my inclining and the rest.
Were it my cue to fight, I should have known it
Without a prompter. Where will you that I go
To answer this your charge?

BRABANTIO   To prison, till fit time
Of law and course of direct session
Call thee to answer.

OTHELLO   What if I do obey?
How may the Duke be therewith satisfied,
Whose messengers are here about my side,
Upon some present business of the state   90
To bring me to him?

OFFICER   'Tis true, most worthy signor:
The Duke's in council, and your noble self
I am sure is sent for.

BRABANTIO   How? The Duke in council?
In this time of the night? Bring him away.
Mine's not an idle cause; the Duke himself,

Or any of my brothers of the state,
Cannot but feel this wrong as 'twere their own:
For if such actions may have passage free,
Bondslaves and pagans shall our statesmen be.   *Exeunt*

I.3   *The Duke and Senators sitting at a table; with lights*
                        and attendants

DUKE
There is no composition in these news
That gives them credit.

FIRST SENATOR   Indeed they are disproportioned.
My letters say a hundred and seven galleys.

DUKE
And mine, a hundred and forty.

SECOND SENATOR   And mine two hundred;
But though they jump not on a just accompt –
As in these cases where the aim reports
'Tis oft with difference – yet do they all confirm
A Turkish fleet, and bearing up to Cyprus.

DUKE
Nay, it is possible enough to judgement:
I do not so secure me in the error,
But the main article I do approve
In fearful sense.

SAILOR (*without*) What, ho! What, ho! What, ho!

FIRST OFFICER
A messenger from the galleys.
                Enter Sailor

DUKE   Now, what's the business?

SAILOR
The Turkish preparation makes for Rhodes;
So was I bid report here to the state
By Signor Angelo.

62

DUKE

How say you by this change?

FIRST SENATOR   This cannot be,

By no assay of reason. 'Tis a pageant
To keep us in false gaze. When we consider
Th'importancy of Cyprus to the Turk,   20
And let ourselves again but understand
That as it more concerns the Turk than Rhodes,
So may he with more facile question bear it,
For that it stands not in such warlike brace,
But altogether lacks th'abilities
That Rhodes is dressed in. If we make thought of this,
We must not think the Turk is so unskilful
To leave that latest which concerns him first,
Neglecting an attempt of ease and gain
To wake and wage a danger profitless.   30

DUKE

Nay, in all confidence he's not for Rhodes.

FIRST OFFICER

Here is more news.

Enter a Messenger

MESSENGER

The Ottomites, reverend and gracious,
Steering with due course toward the isle of Rhodes,
Have there injointed with an after fleet.

FIRST SENATOR

Ay, so I thought. How many, as you guess?

MESSENGER

Of thirty sail; and now they do re-stem
Their backward course, bearing with frank appearance
Their purposes toward Cyprus. Signor Montano,
Your trusty and most valiant servitor,   40
With his free duty recommends you thus,
And prays you to believe him.

63

DUKE

'Tis certain then for Cyprus.

Marcus Luccicos, is not he in town?

FIRST SENATOR

He's now in Florence.

DUKE   Write from us: wish him

Post-post-haste dispatch.

FIRST SENATOR

Here comes Brabantio and the valiant Moor.

Enter Brabantio, Othello, Iago, Roderigo, and
officers

DUKE

Valiant Othello, we must straight employ you

Against the general enemy Ottoman.

50   (*To Brabantio*) I did not see you: welcome, gentle signor;

We lacked your counsel and your help tonight.

BRABANTIO

So did I yours. Good your grace, pardon me:

Neither my place, nor aught I heard of business,

Hath raised me from my bed; nor doth the general care

Take hold on me; for my particular grief

Is of so flood-gate and o'erbearing nature

That it engluts and swallows other sorrows

And yet is still itself.

DUKE   Why? What's the matter?

BRABANTIO

My daughter! O, my daughter!

SENATORS   Dead?

BRABANTIO   Ay, to me.

60   She is abused, stolen from me, and corrupted

By spells and medicines bought of mountebanks;

For nature so preposterously to err,

Being not deficient, blind, or lame of sense,

Sans witchcraft could not.

64

DUKE

  Whoe'er he be that in this foul proceeding
  Hath thus beguiled your daughter of herself
  And you of her, the bloody book of law
  You shall yourself read in the bitter letter *own*
  After your own sense, yea, though our proper son
  Stood in your action.

BRABANTIO   Humbly I thank your grace.   70

  Here is the man: this Moor, whom now it seems
  Your special mandate for the state affairs
  Hath hither brought.

ALL   We are very sorry for't.

DUKE

  What in your own part can you say to this?

BRABANTIO

  Nothing, but this is so.

OTHELLO

  Most potent, grave and reverend signors,
  My very noble and approved good masters,
  That I have ta'en away this old man's daughter,
  It is most true; true I have married her;
  The very head and front of my offending   80
  Hath this extent, no more. Rude am I in my speech
  And little blessed with the soft phrase of peace; *f an ap 7*
  For since these arms of mine had seven years' pith *until*
  Till now some nine moons wasted, they have used *9 months*
  Their dearest action in the tented field; *ago*
  And little of this great world can I speak
  More than pertains to feats of broil and battle;
  And therefore little shall I grace my cause
  In speaking for myself. Yet, by your gracious patience,
  I will a round unvarnished tale deliver   90
  Of my whole course of love: what drugs, what charms,

What conjuration and what mighty magic –
For such proceedings I am charged withal –
I won his daughter.

BRABANTIO   A maiden never bold;
Of spirit so still and quiet that her motion
Blushed at herself: and she, in spite of nature,
Of years, of country, credit, everything,
To fall in love with what she feared to look on!
It is a judgement maimed and most imperfect
That will confess perfection so could err
Against all rules of nature, and must be driven
To find out practices of cunning hell
Why this should be. I therefore vouch again
That with some mixtures powerful o'er the blood,
Or with some dram conjured to this effect,
He wrought upon her.

DUKE   To vouch this is no proof,
Without more wider and more overt test
Than these thin habits and poor likelihoods
Of modern seeming do prefer against him.

FIRST SENATOR
But, Othello, speak:
Did you by indirect and forcèd courses
Subdue and poison this young maid's affections?
Or came it by request and such fair question
As soul to soul affordeth?

OTHELLO   I do beseech you,
Send for the lady to the Sagittary,
And let her speak of me before her father.
If you do find me foul in her report,
The trust, the office I do hold of you
Not only take away, but let your sentence
Even fall upon my life.

DUKE   Fetch Desdemona hither.

OTHELLO

    Ancient, conduct them: you best know the place.

                         Exit Iago with attendants

    And till she come, as truly as to heaven
    I do confess the vices of my blood,
    So justly to your grave ears I'll present
    How I did thrive in this fair lady's love,
    And she in mine.

DUKE   Say it, Othello.

OTHELLO

    Her father loved me, oft invited me,
    Still questioned me the story of my life
    From year to year – the battles, sieges, fortunes
    That I have passed.   130
    I ran it through, even from my boyish days
    To th'very moment that he bade me tell it:
    Wherein I spake of most disastrous chances,
    Of moving accidents by flood and field,
    Of hair-breadth scapes i'th'imminent deadly breach,
    Of being taken by the insolent foe,
    And sold to slavery; of my redemption thence,
    And portance in my travels' history:
    Wherein of antres vast and deserts idle,
    Rough quarries, rocks, and hills whose heads touch   140
            heaven,
    It was my hint to speak – such was the process:
    And of the Cannibals that each other eat,
    The Anthropophagi, and men whose heads
    Do grow beneath their shoulders. This to hear
    Would Desdemona seriously incline:
    But still the house affairs would draw her thence,
    Which ever as she could with haste dispatch
    She'd come again, and with a greedy ear
    Devour up my discourse; which I observing

150 Took once a pliant hour, and found good means
To draw from her a prayer of earnest heart
That I would all my pilgrimage dilate
Whereof by parcels she had something heard,
But not intentively. I did consent,
And often did beguile her of her tears
When I did speak of some distressful stroke
That my youth suffered. My story being done,
She gave me for my pains a world of sighs:
She swore, in faith 'twas strange, 'twas passing strange,
160 'Twas pitiful, 'twas wondrous pitiful;
She wished she had not heard it, yet she wished
That heaven had made her such a man. She thanked me,
And bade me, if I had a friend that loved her,
I should but teach him how to tell my story,
And that would woo her. Upon this hint I spake:
She loved me for the dangers I had passed,
And I loved her, that she did pity them.
This only is the witchcraft I have used.
Here comes the lady: let her witness it.

Enter Desdemona, Iago, and attendants

DUKE
170 I think this tale would win my daughter too.
Good Brabantio, take up this mangled matter at the best:
Men do their broken weapons rather use
Than their bare hands.

BRABANTIO   I pray you hear her speak.
If she confess that she was half the wooer,
Destruction on my head, if my bad blame
Light on the man! Come hither, gentle mistress;
Do you perceive in all this company
Where most you owe obedience?

DESDEMONA   My noble father,
I do perceive here a divided duty:

68

To you I am bound for life and education;   180
My life and education both do learn me
How to respect you. You are lord of all my duty,
I am hitherto your daughter. But here's my husband;
And so much duty as my mother showed
To you, preferring you before her father,
So much I challenge, that I may profess
Due to the Moor, my lord.

BRABANTIO   God bu'y! I have done.
Please it your grace, on to the state affairs.
I had rather to adopt a child than get it.
Come hither, Moor: 190
I here do give thee that with all my heart
Which, but thou hast already, with all my heart
I would keep from thee. For your sake, jewel,
I am glad at soul I have no other child,
For thy escape would teach me tyranny
To hang clogs on them. I have done, my lord.

DUKE
Let me speak like yourself and lay a sentence
Which as a grise or step may help these lovers
Into your favour.
When remedies are past the griefs are ended   200
By seeing the worst which late on hopes depended.
To mourn a mischief that is past and gone
Is the next way to draw new mischief on.
What cannot be preserved when fortune takes,
Patience her injury a mockery makes.
The robbed that smiles steals something from the thief,
He robs himself that spends a bootless grief.

BRABANTIO
So let the Turk of Cyprus us beguile,
We lose it not so long as we can smile;
He bears the sentence well that nothing bears   210

69

I.3

But the free comfort which from thence he hears;
But he bears both the sentence and the sorrow
That to pay grief must of poor patience borrow.
These sentences, to sugar or to gall
Being strong on both sides, are equivocal.
But words are words; I never yet did hear
That the bruised heart was piecèd through the ear.
I humbly beseech you proceed to th'affairs of state.

DUKE The Turk with a most mighty preparation makes for
Cyprus. Othello, the fortitude of the place is best known
to you: and though we have there a substitute of most
allowed sufficiency, yet opinion, a more sovereign mistress of effects, throws a more safer voice on you. You
must therefore be content to slubber the gloss of your
new fortunes with this more stubborn and boisterous
expedition.

OTHELLO
The tyrant, custom, most grave Senators,
Hath made the flinty and steel couch of war
My thrice-driven bed of down. I do agnize
A natural and prompt alacrity
I find in hardness; and do undertake
This present war against the Ottomites.
Most humbly, therefore, bending to your state,
I crave fit disposition for my wife,
Due reference of place and exhibition,
With such accommodation and besort
As levels with her breeding.

DUKE   If you please,
Be't at her father's.

BRABANTIO   I'll not have it so.

OTHELLO
Nor I.

DESDEMONA Nor I: I would not there reside

70

To put my father in impatient thoughts   240
By being in his eye. Most gracious Duke,
To my unfolding lend your prosperous ear,
And let me find a charter in your voice
T'assist my simpleness.

DUKE   What would you? Speak.

DESDEMONA
That I did love the Moor to live with him,
My downright violence and storm of fortunes
May trumpet to the world. My heart's subdued
Even to the very quality of my lord.
I saw Othello's visage in his mind
And to his honours and his valiant parts   250
Did I my soul and fortunes consecrate.
So that, dear lords, if I be left behind
A moth of peace, and he go to the war,
The rites for which I love him are bereft me,
And I a heavy interim shall support
By his dear absence. Let me go with him.

OTHELLO
Let her have your voice.
Vouch with me, heaven, I therefore beg it not
To please the palate of my appetite,
Nor to comply with heat – the young affects   260
In me defunct – and proper satisfaction;
But to be free and bounteous to her mind.
And heaven defend your good souls that you think
I will your serious and great business scant
For she is with me. No, when light-winged toys
Of feathered Cupid seel with wanton dullness
My speculative and officed instruments,
That my disports corrupt and taint my business,
Let housewives make a skillet of my helm,
And all indign and base adversities   270

Make head against my estimation!

DUKE

Be it as you shall privately determine,
Either for her stay, or going. Th'affair cries haste,
And speed must answer it. You must hence tonight.

DESDEMONA

Tonight, my lord? *their wedding night.*

DUKE   This night.

OTHELLO   With all my heart.

DUKE

At nine i'th'morning, here we'll meet again.
Othello, leave some officer behind,
And he shall our commission bring to you,
With such things else of quality and respect
280   As doth import you.   *Iago.*

OTHELLO   So please your grace, my Ancient.

A man he is of honesty and trust:
To his conveyance I assign my wife,
With what else needful your good grace shall think
To be sent after me.

DUKE   Let it be so.

Good night to everyone. And, noble signor,
If virtue no delighted beauty lack,
Your son-in-law is far more fair than black.

FIRST SENATOR

Adieu, brave Moor: use Desdemona well.

BRABANTIO

Look to her, Moor, if thou hast eyes to see.
290   She has deceived her father, and may thee.

OTHELLO

My life upon her faith!
                    Exeunt Duke, Senators, and attendants
                    Honest Iago,
My Desdemona must I leave to thee.

I prithee let thy wife attend on her, *Emilia*
And bring them after in the best advantage.
Come, Desdemona, I have but an hour
Of love, of worldly matters and direction
To spend with thee. We must obey the time.

START HERE *Exeunt Othello and Desdemona*

NOV 3.

RODERIGO Iago.

IAGO What say'st thou, <u>noble heart</u>? sarcasm

RODERIGO What will I do, think'st thou?

IAGO Why, go to bed and sleep.

RODERIGO I will incontinently drown myself. Infatuated with D.

IAGO If thou dost, I shall never love thee after. Why, thou <u>silly gentleman</u>! reverse of 'noble heart'

RODERIGO It is silliness to live, when to live is torment: and then we have a prescription to die, when death is our physician.

IAGO O villainous! I have looked upon the world for four times seven years, and since I could distinguish betwixt a benefit and an injury, I never found a man that knew how to love himself. Ere I would say I would drown myself for the love of a <u>guinea-hen</u>, I would change my humanity with a baboon. prostitute

RODERIGO What should I do? I confess it is my shame to be so fond, but it is not in my virtue to amend it.

IAGO Virtue? A fig! 'Tis in ourselves that we are thus, or thus. <u>Our bodies are our gardens, to the which our wills are gardeners.</u> So that if we will plant nettles or sow lettuce, set hyssop and weed up thyme, supply it with one gender of herbs or distract it with many, either to have it sterile with idleness or manured with industry, why the power and corrigible authority of this lies in our <u>wills</u>. If the beam of our lives had not one scale of reason to poise another of sensuality, the blood and baseness of our natures would conduct us to most

28

310

320

sexual oath

sermon

balance

preposterous conclusions. But we have reason to cool
our raging motions, our carnal stings, our unbitted lusts:
whereof I take this, that you call love, to be a sect or
scion.

330 RODERIGO It cannot be.

IAGO It is merely a lust of the blood and a permission of
the will. Come, be a man. Drown thyself? Drown cats
and blind puppies. I have professed me thy friend, and
I confess me knit to thy deserving with cables of perdurable toughness. I could never better stead thee than
now. Put money in thy purse. Follow thou these wars;
defeat thy favour with an usurped beard. I say, put
money in thy purse. It cannot be that Desdemona should
long continue her love to the Moor – put money in thy
340 purse – nor he his to her. It was a violent commence-
ment, and thou shalt see an answerable sequestration –
put but money in thy purse. These Moors are change-
able in their wills – fill thy purse with money. The food
that to him now is as luscious as locusts shall be to him
shortly as acerbe as the coloquintida. She must change
for youth: when she is sated with his body she will find
the error of her choice. Therefore put money in thy
purse. If thou wilt needs damn thyself, do it a more
delicate way than drowning. Make all the money thou
350 canst. If sanctimony and a frail vow betwixt an erring
barbarian and a super-subtle Venetian be not too hard
for my wits and all the tribe of hell, thou shalt enjoy
her – therefore make money. A pox of drowning thyself!
It is clean out of the way. Seek thou rather to be hanged
in compassing thy joy than to be drowned and go without her.

RODERIGO Wilt thou be fast to my hopes, if I depend on
the issue?

IAGO Thou art sure of me. Go make money. I have told

74

thee often, and I re-tell thee again and again, I hate 360
the Moor. My cause is hearted: thine hath no less
reason. Let us be conjunctive in our revenge against
him. If thou canst cuckold him, thou dost thyself a
pleasure, me a sport. There are many events in the
womb of time, which will be delivered. Traverse! Go,
provide thy money. We will have more of this tomorrow.
Adieu.

RODERIGO Where shall we meet i'th'morning?

IAGO At my lodging.

RODERIGO I'll be with thee betimes. 370

IAGO Go to; farewell. Do you hear, Roderigo?

RODERIGO What say you?

IAGO No more of drowning, do you hear?

RODERIGO I am changed.

IAGO Go to; farewell. Put money enough in your purse.

RODERIGO I'll sell all my land. *Exit*

IAGO

Thus do I ever make my fool my purse:
For I mine own gained knowledge should profane
If I would time expend with such a snipe
But for my sport and profit. I hate the Moor, 380
And it is thought abroad that 'twixt my sheets
He's done my office. I know not if't be true
But I, for mere suspicion in that kind,
Will do as if for surety. He holds me well:
The better shall my purpose work on him.
Cassio's a proper man: let me see now;
To get his place and to plume up my will
In double knavery. How? How? Let's see.
After some time, to abuse Othello's ear
That he is too familiar with his wife; 390
He hath a person and a smooth dispose
To be suspected, framed to make women false.

75

The Moor is of a free and open nature,
That thinks men honest that but seem to be so,
And will as tenderly be led by th'nose
As asses are.
I have't. It is engendered. Hell and night
Must bring this monstrous birth to the world's light.

Exit

*

In Cyprus from now on. After Battle with Turkish fleet

II.1   *Enter Montano and two Gentlemen*

MONTANO
What from the cape can you discern at sea?

FIRST GENTLEMAN
Nothing at all; it is a high-wrought flood.
I cannot 'twixt the heaven and the main
Descry a sail.

MONTANO
Methinks the wind does speak aloud at land;
A fuller blast ne'er shook our battlements.
If it hath ruffianed so upon the sea,
What ribs of oak, when mountains melt on them,
Can hold the mortise? What shall we hear of this?

SECOND GENTLEMAN
10   A segregation of the Turkish fleet: *cursing*
For do but stand upon the banning shore,
The chidden billow seems to pelt the clouds;
The wind-shaked surge, with high and monstrous mane,
Seems to cast water on the burning Bear
And quench the guards of th'ever-fixèd Pole.
I never did like molestation view
On the enchafèd flood.

MONTANO   If that the Turkish fleet
Be not ensheltered and embayed, they are drowned:
It is impossible they bear it out.

Enter a Gentleman

THIRD GENTLEMAN
News, lads! Our wars are done: 20
The desperate tempest hath so banged the Turks
That their designment halts. A noble ship of Venice
Hath seen a grievous wrack and sufferance
On most part of their fleet.

MONTANO
How! Is this true?

THIRD GENTLEMAN The ship is here put in,
A Veronesa; Michael Cassio,
Lieutenant to the warlike Moor, Othello,
Is come on shore; the Moor himself at sea,
And is in full commission here for Cyprus. *as governor.*

MONTANO
I am glad on't; 'tis a worthy governor.   30

THIRD GENTLEMAN
But this same Cassio, though he speak of comfort
Touching the Turkish loss, yet he looks sadly *note. in view of*
And prays the Moor be safe; for they were parted *O's future*
With foul and violent tempest.   *view of Cassio.*

MONTANO   Pray heaven he be:
For I have served him, and the man commands
Like a full soldier. Let's to the sea-side, ho!
As well to see the vessel that's come in,
As to throw out our eyes for brave Othello,
Even till we make the main and th'aerial blue
An indistinct regard.

THIRD GENTLEMAN   Come, let's do so;   40
For every minute is expectancy
Of more arrivance.
          Enter Cassio

CASSIO
Thanks, you the valiant of this warlike isle

77

That so approve the Moor! O, let the heavens
Give him defence against the elements,
For I have lost him on a dangerous sea.

MONTANO
Is he well shipped?

CASSIO
His bark is stoutly timbered, and his pilot
Of very expert and approved allowance;
50 Therefore my hopes, not surfeited to death,
Stand in bold cure.
            (*Cry within* 'A sail, a sail, a sail!')

CASSIO
What noise?

FOURTH GENTLEMAN
The town is empty; on the brow o'th'sea
Stand ranks of people, and they cry 'A sail!'

CASSIO
My hopes do shape him for the Governor.
        Salvo

SECOND GENTLEMAN
They do discharge their shot of courtesy:
Our friends at least.

CASSIO   I pray you, sir, go forth,
And give us truth who 'tis that is arrived.

SECOND GENTLEMAN
I shall.   *Exit*

MONTANO
60 But, good Lieutenant, is your General wived?

CASSIO
Most fortunately: he hath achieved a maid
That paragons description and wild fame;
One that excels the quirks of blazoning pens,
And in th'essential vesture of creation
Does tire the ingener.

78

Enter Second Gentleman
                    How now? Who has put in?

SECOND GENTLEMAN
  'Tis one Iago, Ancient to the General.

CASSIO
  He's had most favourable and happy speed:
  Tempests themselves, high seas, and howling winds,
  The guttered rocks and congregated sands,
  Traitors enscarped to clog the guiltless keel,
  As having sense of beauty, do omit
  Their mortal natures, letting go safely by
  The divine Desdemona.

MONTANO   What is she?

CASSIO
  She that I spake of, our great Captain's Captain,
  Left in the conduct of the bold Iago,
  Whose footing here anticipates our thoughts
  A se'nnight's speed. Great Jove, Othello guard,
  And swell his sail with thine own powerful breath,
  That he may bless this bay with his tall ship,
  Make love's quick pants in Desdemona's arms,
  Give renewed fire to our extinct spirits,
  And bring all Cyprus comfort.
      Enter Desdemona, Emilia, Iago, Roderigo, and attendants
                      O, behold,
  The riches of the ship is come on shore!
  You men of Cyprus, let her have your knees.
  Hail to thee, lady! And the grace of heaven,
  Before, behind thee, and on every hand,
  Enwheel thee round.

DESDEMONA   I thank you, valiant Cassio.
  What tidings can you tell me of my lord?

CASSIO
  He is not yet arrived; nor know I aught

90   But that he's well, and will be shortly here.

DESDEMONA

O, but I fear! How lost you company?

CASSIO

The great contention of the sea and skies
Parted our fellowship.
        (*Cry within*) 'A sail, a sail!'
                            But hark, a sail!

GENTLEMAN

They give their greeting to the citadel:
This likewise is a friend.

CASSIO   See for the news.

Good Ancient, you are welcome. Welcome, mistress.
Let it not gall your patience, good Iago,
That I extend my manners. 'Tis my breeding
That gives me this bold show of courtesy.
        He kisses Emilia

IAGO

100 Sir, would she give you so much of her lips
As of her tongue she oft bestows on me,
You'd have enough.

DESDEMONA

Alas, she has no speech.

IAGO   In faith, too much.

I find it still when I have list to sleep.
Marry, before your ladyship, I grant
She puts her tongue a little in her heart
And chides with thinking.

EMILIA   You have little cause to say so.

IAGO Come on, come on: you are pictures out of doors,
bells in your parlours, wild-cats in your kitchens, saints
110 in your injuries, devils being offended, players in your
housewifery, and housewives in your beds.

DESDEMONA

O, fie upon thee, slanderer!

IAGO

Nay, it is true, or else I am a Turk:
You rise to play and go to bed to work.

insulting bitter

EMILIA

You shall not write my praise.

IAGO   No, let me not.

DESDEMONA

What wouldst thou write of me, if thou shouldst praise
      me?

IAGO

O, gentle lady, do not put me to't,
For I am nothing if not critical.

DESDEMONA

Come on, assay. There's one gone to the harbour?

IAGO

Ay, madam.   120

DESDEMONA

(*aside*) I am not merry, but I do beguile
The thing I am by seeming otherwise.
Come, how wouldst thou praise me?

IAGO

I am about it, but indeed my invention
Comes from my pate as birdlime does from frieze – *material*
It plucks out brains and all. But my muse labours,
And thus she is delivered.
If she be fair and wise, fairness and wit,
The one's for use, the other useth it.

DESDEMONA

Well praised! How if she be black and witty?   130

IAGO

If she be black, and thereto have a wit,
She'll find a white that shall her blackness fit.

81

II.1

DESDEMONA
Worse and worse.

EMILIA   How if fair and foolish?

IAGO
She never yet was foolish that was fair,
For even her folly helped her to an heir.

DESDEMONA These are old fond paradoxes to make fools
laugh i'th'alehouse. What miserable praise hast thou for
her that's foul and foolish?

IAGO
There's none so foul and foolish thereunto,
140   But does foul pranks which fair and wise ones do.

DESDEMONA O heavy ignorance! Thou praisest the worst
best. But what praise couldst thou bestow on a deserving
woman indeed? One that in the authority of her merit
did justly put on the vouch of very malice itself?

IAGO
She that was ever fair and never proud,
Had tongue at will, and yet was never loud;
Never lacked gold, and yet went never gay;
Fled from her wish, and yet said 'Now I may';
She that being angered, her revenge being nigh,
150   Bade her wrong stay, and her displeasure fly;
She that in wisdom never was so frail
To change the cod's head for the salmon's tail;
She that could think and ne'er disclose her mind:
See suitors following and not look behind:
She was a wight, if ever such wight were –

DESDEMONA
To do what?

IAGO
To suckle fools and chronicle small beer.

DESDEMONA
O, most lame and impotent conclusion!

Do not learn of him, Emilia, though he be thy husband.
How say you, Cassio, is he not a most profane and 160
liberal counsellor?

CASSIO He speaks home, madam; you may relish him more
in the soldier than in the scholar.

IAGO (*aside*) He takes her by the palm. Ay, well said,
whisper. With as little a web as this will I ensnare as
great a fly as Cassio. Ay, smile upon her, do. I will
gyve thee in thine own courtship. You say true, 'tis so
indeed. If such tricks as these strip you out of your
lieutenantry, it had been better you had not kissed your
three fingers so oft, which now again you are most apt 170
to play the sir in. Very good: well kissed, an excellent
courtesy! 'Tis so indeed. Yet again your fingers to your
lips? Would they were clyster-pipes for your sake!

　　Trumpet

(*aloud*) The Moor! I know his trumpet.

CASSIO　　　　　　　　　　　　　'Tis truly so.

DESDEMONA

Let's meet him and receive him.

CASSIO　　　　　　　　　　　Lo, where he comes!
　　Enter Othello and attendants

OTHELLO

O, my fair warrior!

DESDEMONA　　　　My dear Othello!

OTHELLO

It gives me wonder great as my content
To see you here before me. O, my soul's joy!
If after every tempest come such calms,
May the winds blow till they have wakened death, 180
And let the labouring bark climb hills of seas,
Olympus-high, and duck again as low
As hell's from heaven. If it were now to die,
'Twere now to be most happy; for I fear

My soul hath her content so absolute
That not another comfort like to this
Succeeds in unknown fate.

DESDEMONA   The heavens forbid
But that our loves and comforts should increase,
Even as our days do grow.

OTHELLO   Amen to that, sweet Powers!

190 I cannot speak enough of this content;
It stops me here; it is too much of joy.
          They kiss
And this, and this the greatest discords be
That e'er our hearts shall make.

IAGO (*aside*)   O, you are well tuned now!
But I'll set down the pegs that make this music,
As honest as I am.

OTHELLO   Come, let's to the castle.
News, friends; our wars are done; the Turks are
          drowned.
How does my old acquaintance of this isle?
Honey, you shall be well desired in Cyprus:
I have found great love amongst them. O my sweet,

200 I prattle out of fashion and I dote
In mine own comforts. I prithee, good Iago,
Go to the bay and disembark my coffers;
Bring thou the Master to the citadel;
He is a good one, and his worthiness
Does challenge much respect. Come, Desdemona,
Once more well met at Cyprus!

                    Exeunt all except Iago and Roderigo

IAGO (*to soldiers, who go off*) Do thou meet me presently at
the harbour. (*To Roderigo*) Come hither. If thou be'st
valiant – as they say base men being in love have then a

210 nobility in their natures more than is native to them –
list me. The Lieutenant tonight watches on the court of

guard. First, I must tell thee this: Desdemona is directly
in love with him.

RODERIGO With him? Why, 'tis not possible!

IAGO Lay thy finger thus, and let thy soul be instructed.
Mark me with what violence she first loved the Moor,
but for bragging and telling her fantastical lies. And
will she love him still for prating? Let not thy discreet
heart think it. Her eye must be fed. And what delight
shall she have to look on the devil? When the blood is 220
made dull with the act of sport, there should be, again
to inflame it and give satiety a fresh appetite, loveliness
in favour, sympathy in years, manners and beauties: all
which the Moor is defective in. Now for want of these
required conveniences, her delicate tenderness will find
itself abused, begin to heave the gorge, disrelish and
abhor the Moor. Very nature will instruct her in it and
compel her to some second choice. Now, sir, this granted
– as it is a most pregnant and unforced position – who
stands so eminently in the degree of this fortune as 230
Cassio does? – a knave very voluble; no further conscionable than in putting on the mere form of civil and
humane seeming for the better compassing of his salt
and most hidden loose affection. Why, none; why, none
– a slipper and subtle knave, a finder out of occasions;
that has an eye can stamp and counterfeit advantages,
though true advantage never present itself; a devilish
knave! Besides, the knave is handsome, young, and hath
all those requisites in him that folly and green minds
look after. A pestilent complete knave; and the woman 240
hath found him already.

RODERIGO I cannot believe that in her: she's full of most
blessed condition.

IAGO Blessed fig's end! The wine she drinks is made of
grapes. If she had been blessed, she would never have

loved the Moor. Blessed pudding! Didst thou not see her
paddle with the palm of his hand? Didst not mark that?

RODERIGO Yes, that I did: but that was but courtesy.

IAGO Lechery, by this hand: an index and obscure prologue to the history of lust and foul thoughts. They met
so near with their lips that their breaths embraced
together. Villainous thoughts, Roderigo! When these
mutualities so marshal the way, hard at hand comes the
master and main exercise, th'incorporate conclusion.
Pish! But, sir, be you ruled by me. I have brought you
from Venice. Watch you tonight: for the command, I'll
lay't upon you. Cassio knows you not; I'll not be far
from you. Do you find some occasion to anger Cassio,
either by speaking too loud, or tainting his discipline, or
from what other course you please, which the time shall
more favourably minister.

RODERIGO Well.

IAGO Sir, he's rash and very sudden in choler, and haply
with his truncheon may strike at you: provoke him that
he may, for even out of that will I cause these of Cyprus
to mutiny, whose qualification shall come into no true
taste again but by the displanting of Cassio. So shall you
have a shorter journey to your desires by the means I
shall then have to prefer them, and the impediment most
profitably removed, without the which there were no
expectation of our prosperity.

RODERIGO I will do this, if you can bring it to any opportunity.

IAGO I warrant thee. Meet me by and by at the citadel. I
must fetch his necessaries ashore. Farewell.

RODERIGO Adieu.   *Exit*

IAGO

That Cassio loves her, I do well believe't:
That she loves him, 'tis apt and of great credit.

290
260
270

The Moor – howbeit that I endure him not –
Is of a constant, loving, noble nature,
And, I dare think, he'll prove to Desdemona   280
A most dear husband. Now, I do love her too;
Not out of absolute lust – though peradventure
I stand accountant for as great a sin –
But partly led to diet my revenge
For that I do suspect the lusty Moor
Hath leaped into my seat, the thought whereof
Doth, like a poisonous mineral, gnaw my inwards,
And nothing can, or shall, content my soul
Till I am evened with him, wife for wife;   290
Or failing so, yet that I put the Moor
At least into a jealousy so strong
That judgement cannot cure. Which thing to do
If this poor trash of Venice, whom I leash   Roderigo
For his quick hunting, stand the putting on,
I'll have our Michael Cassio on the hip,
Abuse him to the Moor in the rank garb –
For I fear Cassio with my night-cap too –
Make the Moor thank me, love me, and reward me
For making him egregiously an ass,   300
And practising upon his peace and quiet,
Even to madness. 'Tis here, but yet confused:
Knavery's plain face is never seen till used.   *Exit*

Enter Herald, with a proclamation   II.2
HERALD It is Othello's pleasure, our noble and valiant
General, that upon certain tidings now arrived importing
the mere perdition of the Turkish fleet, every man put
himself into triumph: some to dance, some to make
bonfires, each man to what sport and revels his addiction
leads him. For, besides these beneficial news, it is the

celebration of his nuptial. So much was his pleasure
should be proclaimed. All offices are open, and there is
full liberty of feasting from this present hour of five
till the bell have told eleven. Heaven bless the isle of
Cyprus and our noble General Othello!   *Exit*

II.3   *Enter Othello, Desdemona, Cassio, and attendants*

OTHELLO
Good Michael, look you to the guard tonight.
Let's teach ourselves that honourable stop,
Not to outsport discretion.

CASSIO
Iago hath direction what to do;
But, notwithstanding, with my personal eye
Will I look to't.

OTHELLO   Iago is most honest.
Michael, good night. Tomorrow with your earliest
Let me have speech with you. (*To Desdemona*) Come,
            my dear love,
The purchase made, the fruits are to ensue:
That profit's yet to come 'tween me and you.
Good night.
            Exeunt Othello, Desdemona, and attendants
            Enter Iago

CASSIO Welcome, Iago; we must to the watch.

IAGO Not this hour, Lieutenant; 'tis not yet ten o'th'clock.
Our General cast us thus early for the love of his
Desdemona; who let us not therefore blame. He hath
not yet made wanton the night with her; and she is
sport for Jove.

CASSIO She is a most exquisite lady.

IAGO And, I'll warrant her, full of game.

CASSIO Indeed, she is a most fresh and delicate creature.

88

IAGO What an eye she has! Methinks it sounds a parley to
provocation.

CASSIO An inviting eye, and yet methinks right modest.

IAGO And when she speaks, is it not an alarum to love?

CASSIO She is indeed perfection.

IAGO Well, happiness to their sheets! Come, Lieutenant,
I have a stoup of wine; and here without are a brace of
Cyprus gallants that would fain have a measure to the
health of black Othello.

CASSIO Not tonight, good Iago. I have very poor and 30
unhappy brains for drinking. I could well wish courtesy
would invent some other custom of entertainment.

IAGO O, they are our friends! But one cup; I'll drink for
you.

CASSIO I have drunk but one cup tonight, and that was
craftily qualified too; and behold what innovation it
makes here. I am unfortunate in the infirmity and dare
not task my weakness with any more.

IAGO What, man! 'Tis a night of revels; the gallants desire
it.   40

CASSIO Where are they?

IAGO Here, at the door: I pray you call them in.

CASSIO I'll do't, but it dislikes me.   *Exit*

IAGO

If I can fasten but one cup upon him,
With that which he hath drunk tonight already,
He'll be as full of quarrel and offence
As my young mistress' dog. Now my sick fool Roderigo,
Whom love hath turned almost the wrong side out,
To Desdemona hath tonight caroused
Potations pottle-deep; and he's to watch.   50
Three else of Cyprus, noble swelling spirits –
That hold their honours in a wary distance,
The very elements of this warlike isle –

Have I tonight flustered with flowing cups,
And they watch too. Now 'mongst this flock of
        drunkards,
Am I to put our Cassio in some action
That may offend the isle. But here they come;
If consequence do but approve my dream,
My boat sails freely both with wind and stream.

*Enter Cassio with Montano and Gentlemen, and
servants with wine*

60 CASSIO 'Fore God, they have given me a rouse already.

MONTANO Good faith, a little one; not past a pint, as I am
a soldier.

IAGO Some wine, ho!

(*sings*)   And let me the canakin clink, clink;
            And let me the canakin clink;
                A soldier's a man
                O, man's life's but a span;
                Why, then, let a soldier drink.

Some wine, boys.

70 CASSIO 'Fore God, an excellent song.

IAGO I learned it in England, where indeed they are most
potent in potting. Your Dane, your German, and your
swag-bellied Hollander – drink, ho! – are nothing to
your English.

CASSIO Is your Englishman so expert in his drinking?

IAGO Why, he drinks you with facility your Dane dead
drunk; he sweats not to overthrow your Almaine; he
gives your Hollander a vomit, ere the next pottle can be
filled.

80 CASSIO To the health of our General!

MONTANO I am for it, Lieutenant; and I'll do you justice.

IAGO O, sweet England!

(*sings*) King Stephen was and-a worthy peer,

His breeches cost him but a crown;
He held them sixpence all too dear;
    With that he called the tailor lown.
He was a wight of high renown,
    And thou art but of low degree;
'Tis pride that pulls the country down;   90
    Then take thine auld cloak about thee.

Some wine, ho!

CASSIO 'Fore God, this is a more exquisite song than the other.

IAGO Will you hear't again?

CASSIO No, for I hold him to be unworthy of his place that does those things. Well, God's above all; and there be souls must be saved, and there be souls must not be saved.

IAGO It's true, good Lieutenant.   100

CASSIO For mine own part – no offence to the General, nor any man of quality – I hope to be saved.

IAGO And so do I too, Lieutenant.

CASSIO Ay, but, by your leave, not before me. The Lieutenant is to be saved before the Ancient. Let's have no more of this; let's to our affairs. God forgive us our sins. Gentlemen, let's look to our business. Do not think, gentlemen, I am drunk: this is my Ancient, this is my right hand, and this is my left. I am not drunk now: I can stand well enough and I speak well enough.   110

GENTLEMEN Excellent well.

CASSIO Why, very well; you must not think then that I am drunk.   *Exit*

MONTANO To th'platform, masters; come, let's set the watch.

IAGO
    You see this fellow that is gone before:
    He is a soldier, fit to stand by Caesar

Casio

And give direction; and do but see his vice:
'Tis to his virtue a just equinox,
120   The one as long as th'other. 'Tis pity of him.
I fear the trust Othello puts in him,
On some odd time of his infirmity,
Will shake this island.

MONTANO   But is he often thus?

IAGO
'Tis evermore the prologue to his sleep:
He'll watch the horologe a double set,
If drink rock not his cradle.

MONTANO   It were well
The General were put in mind of it:
Perhaps he sees it not, or his good nature
Prizes the virtue that appears in Cassio
130   And looks not on his evils. Is not this true?

          Enter Roderigo

IAGO
(*aside*) How now, Roderigo!
I pray you after the Lieutenant go!   *Exit Roderigo*

MONTANO
And 'tis great pity that the noble Moor
Should hazard such a place as his own second
With one of an ingraft infirmity.
It were an honest action to say
So to the Moor.

IAGO   Not I, for this fair island!
I do love Cassio well and would do much
To cure him of this evil.
          (*Cry within*) 'Help! Help!'
                    But hark, what noise?

          Enter Cassio, pursuing Roderigo

CASSIO Zounds, you rogue, you rascal!
MONTANO What's the matter, Lieutenant?

92

CASSIO A knave teach me my duty? I'll beat the knave into a twiggen-bottle.

RODERIGO Beat me?

CASSIO Dost thou prate, rogue?

 He strikes Roderigo

MONTANO Nay, good Lieutenant; I pray you, sir, hold your hand.

CASSIO Let me go, sir, or I'll knock you o'er the mazzard.

MONTANO Come, come, you're drunk.

CASSIO Drunk!   150

IAGO (*to Roderigo*) Away, I say; go out and cry a mutiny.

          Exit Roderigo

 Nay, good Lieutenant. God's will, gentleman!
 Help, ho! Lieutenant! Sir! Montano! Sir!
 Help, masters. Here's a goodly watch indeed.
  Bell rings
 Who's that which rings the bell? Diablo, ho!
 The town will rise. God's will, Lieutenant, hold!
 You will be shamed for ever!
  Enter Othello and attendants

OTHELLO
 What is the matter here?

MONTANO   Zounds, I bleed still.
 I am hurt to th'death.

OTHELLO   Hold for your lives!

IAGO
 Hold, ho, Lieutenant, sir, Montano, gentlemen!
 Have you forgot all sense of place and duty?
 Hold! The General speaks to you: hold, for shame!

OTHELLO
 Why, how now, ho! From whence ariseth this?
 Are we turned Turks and to ourselves do that
 Which heaven hath forbid the Ottomites?
 For Christian shame, put by this barbarous brawl.

He that stirs next to carve for his own rage
Holds his soul light: he dies upon his motion.
Silence that dreadful bell: it frights the isle
170 From her propriety. What is the matter, masters?
Honest Iago, that looks dead with grieving,
Speak, who began this? On thy love I charge thee.

IAGO

I do not know. Friends all but now, even now,
In quarter and in terms like bride and groom
Devesting them for bed: and then but now –
As if some planet had unwitted men –
Swords out, and tilting one at others' breasts
In opposition bloody. I cannot speak
Any beginning to this peevish odds;
180 And would in action glorious I had lost
Those legs that brought me to a part of it.

OTHELLO

How comes it, Michael, you are thus forgot?

CASSIO

I pray you pardon me: I cannot speak.

OTHELLO

Worthy Montano, you were wont to be civil:
The gravity and stillness of your youth
The world hath noted; and your name is great
In mouths of wisest censure. What's the matter
That you unlace your reputation thus
And spend your rich opinion for the name
190 Of a night-brawler? Give me answer to it.

MONTANO

Worthy Othello, I am hurt to danger.
Your officer, Iago, can inform you,
While I spare speech, which something now offends me,
Of all that I do know; nor know I aught
By me that's said or done amiss this night,

94

Unless self-charity be sometimes a vice,
And to defend ourselves it be a sin
When violence assails us.

OTHELLO   Now, by heaven,
My blood begins my safer guides to rule,
And passion, having my best judgement collied,   200
Assays to lead the way. Zounds, if I stir,
Or do but lift this arm, the best of you
Shall sink in my rebuke. Give me to know
How this foul rout began, who set it on;
And he that is approved in this offence,
Though he had twinned with me, both at a birth,
Shall lose me. What! In a town of war
Yet wild, the people's hearts brimful of fear,   *of the Turks.*
To manage private and domestic quarrel
In night, and on the court and guard of safety,   210
'Tis monstrous. Iago, who began't?

MONTANO
If partially affined or leagued in office,
Thou dost deliver more or less than truth,
Thou art no soldier.

IAGO   Touch me not so near.
I had rather have this tongue cut from my mouth
Than it should do offence to Michael Cassio.
Yet, I persuade myself, to speak the truth
Shall nothing wrong him. This it is, General.
Montano and myself being in speech,
There comes a fellow, crying out for help,   220
And Cassio following with determined sword
To execute upon him. Sir, this gentleman
Steps in to Cassio and entreats his pause:
Myself the crying fellow did pursue
Lest by his clamour – as it so fell out –
The town might fall in fright. He, swift of foot,   *Iago had set Roderigo on to provoke Cassio & disappear so that Cassio thinks Montano attacked him*

Outran my purpose and I returned the rather
For that I heard the clink and fall of swords
And Cassio high in oath, which till tonight
230 I ne'er might say before. When I came back –
For this was brief – I found them close together
At blow and thrust, even as again they were
When you yourself did part them.
More of this matter can I not report:
But men are men; the best sometimes forget.
Though Cassio did some little wrong to him,
As men in rage strike those that wish them best,
Yet surely Cassio, I believe, received
From him that fled some strange indignity
240 Which patience could not pass.

OTHELLO   I know, Iago,
Thy honesty and love doth mince this matter,
Making it light to Cassio. Cassio, I love thee,
But nevermore be officer of mine.   STOP TAPE

Enter Desdemona, attended

Look, if my gentle love be not raised up.
I'll make thee an example.

DESDEMONA   What is the matter, dear?

OTHELLO
All's well now, sweeting: come away to bed.
Sir, for your hurts myself will be your surgeon.

Montano is led off

Iago, look with care about the town
And silence those whom this vile brawl distracted.
250 Come, Desdemona, 'tis the soldiers' life
To have their balmy slumbers waked with strife.

Exeunt all but Iago and Cassio

IAGO What, are you hurt, Lieutenant?
CASSIO Ay, past all surgery.
IAGO Marry, God forbid!

96

CASSIO Reputation, reputation, reputation! O, I have lost
my reputation! I have lost the immortal part of myself,
and what remains is bestial. My reputation, Iago, my
reputation!

IAGO As I am an honest man I thought you had received
some bodily wound: there is more of sense in that 260
than in reputation. Reputation is an idle and most false
imposition; oft got without merit and lost without
deserving. You have lost no reputation at all, unless you
repute yourself such a loser. What, man! There are
ways to recover the General again. You are but now cast
in his mood – a punishment more in policy than in
malice – even so as one would beat his offenceless dog to
affright an imperious lion. Sue to him again, and he's
yours.

CASSIO I will rather sue to be despised than to deceive so 270
good a commander with so slight, so drunken, and so
indiscreet an officer. Drunk! And speak parrot! And
squabble! Swagger! Swear! And discourse fustian with
one's own shadow! O, thou invisible spirit of wine, if
thou hast no name to be known by, let us call thee devil.

IAGO What was he that you followed with your sword?
What had he done to you?

CASSIO I know not.

IAGO Is't possible?

CASSIO I remember a mass of things, but nothing dis- 280
tinctly: a quarrel, but nothing wherefore. O God, that
men should put an enemy in their mouths to steal away
their brains! That we should with joy, pleasance, revel
and applause transform ourselves into beasts!

IAGO Why, but you are now well enough! How came you
thus recovered?

CASSIO It hath pleased the devil drunkenness to give place
to the devil wrath: one unperfectness shows me another,

to make me frankly despise myself.

290 IAGO Come, you are too severe a moraller. As the time, the place and the condition of this country stands, I could heartily wish this had not so befallen: but since it is as it is, mend it for your own good.

CASSIO I will ask him for my place again; he shall tell me I am a drunkard. Had I as many mouths as Hydra, such an answer would stop them all. To be now a sensible man, by and by a fool, and presently a beast! O, strange! Every inordinate cup is unblessed and the ingredience is a devil.

300 IAGO Come, come; good wine is a good familiar creature if it be well used: exclaim no more against it. And, good Lieutenant, I think you think I love you.

CASSIO I have well approved it, sir. I drunk!

IAGO You or any man living may be drunk at a time, man. I'll tell you what you shall do. Our General's wife is now the General. I may say so in this respect, for that he hath devoted and given up himself to the contemplation, mark, and denotement of her parts and graces. Confess yourself freely to her; importune her help to
310 put you in your place again. She is of so free, so kind, so apt, so blessed a disposition, that she holds it a vice in her goodness not to do more than she is requested. This broken joint between you and her husband, entreat her to splinter; and my fortunes against any lay worth naming, this crack of your love shall grow stronger than it was before.

CASSIO You advise me well.

IAGO I protest in the sincerity of love and honest kindness.

320 CASSIO I think it freely; and betimes in the morning I will beseech the virtuous Desdemona to undertake for me. I am desperate of my fortunes if they check me here.

98

IAGO You are in the right. Good night, Lieutenant, I must
   to the watch.

CASSIO Good night, honest Iago.   *Exit*

IAGO
   And what's he then that says I play the villain,
   When this advice is free I give, and honest,
   Probal to thinking, and indeed the course
   To win the Moor again? For 'tis most easy
   Th'inclining Desdemona to subdue   330
   In any honest suit. She's framed as fruitful
   As the free elements; and then for her
   To win the Moor, were't to renounce his baptism,
   All seals and symbols of redeemèd sin,
   His soul is so enfettered to her love,
   That she may make, unmake, do what she list,
   Even as her appetite shall play the god
   With his weak function. How am I then a villain
   To counsel Cassio to this parallel course
   Directly to his good? Divinity of hell!   340
   When devils will the blackest sins put on,
   They do suggest at first with heavenly shows
   As I do now. For whiles this honest fool
   Plies Desdemona to repair his fortunes
   And she for him pleads strongly to the Moor,
   I'll pour this pestilence into his ear:
   That she repeals him for her body's lust,
   And by how much she strives to do him good,
   She shall undo her credit with the Moor.
   So will I turn her virtue into pitch,   350
   And out of her own goodness make the net
   That shall enmesh them all.
        Enter Roderigo
                          How now, Roderigo?

RODERIGO I do follow here in the chase, not like a hound

99

Begins to see the light [handwritten]

pock [handwritten]

that hunts, but one that fills up the cry. My money is
almost spent; I have been tonight exceedingly well
cudgelled; and I think the issue will be, I shall have so
much experience for my pains; and so, with no money
at all, and a little more wit, return again to Venice.

IAGO

How poor are they that have not patience!

360   What wound did ever heal but by degrees?

reinforcing his control [handwritten]

Thou know'st we work by wit, and not by witchcraft,
And wit depends on dilatory time.
Does't not go well? Cassio hath beaten thee,
And thou by that small hurt hath cashiered Cassio.
Though other things grow fair against the sun,
Yet fruits that blossom first will first be ripe.
Content thyself awhile. By th'mass, 'tis morning:
Pleasure and action make the hours seem short.
Retire thee; go where thou art billeted.

370   Away, I say, thou shalt know more hereafter:

Contempt [handwritten]

Nay, get thee gone.   *Exit Roderigo*
                    Two things are to be done.
My wife must move for Cassio to her mistress:
I'll set her on.
Myself the while to draw the Moor apart,
And bring him jump when he may Cassio find
Soliciting his wife. Ay, that's the way.
Dull not device by coldness and delay.   *Exit*

*

III.1   *Enter Cassio and Musicians*

CASSIO

Masters, play here – I will content your pains –
Something that's brief; and bid 'Good morrow, General'.

They play
Enter Clown

CLOWN Why, masters, have your instruments been in
Naples, that they speak i'th'nose thus?

FIRST MUSICIAN How, sir, how?

CLOWN Are these, I pray you, wind instruments?

FIRST MUSICIAN Ay, marry are they, sir.

CLOWN O, thereby hangs a tail.

FIRST MUSICIAN Whereby hangs a tale, sir?

CLOWN Marry, sir, by many a wind instrument that I 10
know. But, masters, here's money for you: and the
General so likes your music that he desires you, for
love's sake, to make no more noise with it.

FIRST MUSICIAN Well, sir, we will not.

CLOWN If you have any music that may not be heard,
to't again. But, as they say, to hear music the General
does not greatly care.

FIRST MUSICIAN We have none such, sir.

CLOWN Then put up your pipes in your bag, for I'll
away. Go, vanish into air, away. *Exeunt Musicians* 20

CASSIO Dost thou hear, mine honest friend?

CLOWN No, I hear not your honest friend: I hear you.

CASSIO Prithee keep up thy quillets – there's a poor piece
of gold for thee. If the gentlewoman that attends the
General's wife be stirring, tell her there's one Cassio
entreats her a little favour of speech. Wilt thou do this?

CLOWN She is stirring, sir. If she will stir hither, I shall
seem to notify unto her.

CASSIO Do, good my friend.   *Exit Clown*
          Enter Iago
In happy time, Iago.

IAGO   You have not been abed then? 30

CASSIO
Why, no: the day had broke before we parted.

101

III.1

I have made bold, Iago,
To send in to your wife. My suit to her
Is that she will to virtuous Desdemona
Procure me some access.

IAGO   I'll send her to you presently;
And I'll devise a mean to draw the Moor
Out of the way, that your converse and business
May be more free.

CASSIO   I humbly thank you for't.

                                  Exit Iago

I never knew a Florentine more kind and honest.
    Enter Emilia

EMILIA
40   Good morrow, good Lieutenant; I am sorry
For your displeasure: but all will sure be well.
The General and his wife are talking of it,
And she speaks for you stoutly. The Moor replies
That he you hurt is of great fame in Cyprus,
And great affinity; and that in wholesome wisdom
He might not but refuse you; but he protests he loves
        you
And needs no other suitor but his likings
To take the safest occasion by the front
To bring you in again.

CASSIO   Yet I beseech you,
50   If you think fit, or that it may be done,
Give me advantage of some brief discourse
With Desdemona alone.

EMILIA   Pray you, come in:
I will bestow you where you shall have time
To speak your bosom freely.

CASSIO   I am much bound to you.
                                      Exeunt

Enter Othello, Iago, and Gentlemen

OTHELLO
These letters give, Iago, to the pilot,
And by him do my duties to the senate.
That done, I will be walking on the works:
Repair there to me.

IAGO   Well, my good lord, I'll do't. *Exit*

OTHELLO
This fortification, gentlemen, shall we see't?

GENTLEMEN
We'll wait upon your lordship.   *Exeunt*

Enter Desdemona, Cassio, and Emilia   III.3

DESDEMONA
Be thou assured, good Cassio, I will do
All my abilities in thy behalf.

EMILIA
Good madam, do: I warrant it grieves my husband
As if the case were his.

DESDEMONA
O, that's an honest fellow! Do not doubt, Cassio,
But I will have my lord and you again
As friendly as you were.

CASSIO   Bounteous madam,
Whatever shall become of Michael Cassio,
He's never anything but your true servant.

DESDEMONA
I know't: I thank you. You do love my lord;   10
You have known him long, and be you well assured
He shall in strangeness stand no farther off
Than in a politic distance.

CASSIO   Ay, but, lady,

That policy may either last so long,
Or feed upon such nice and waterish diet,
Or breed itself so out of circumstance,
That I being absent and my place supplied,
My General will forget my love and service.

DESDEMONA

Do not doubt that. Before Emilia here,
20   I give thee warrant of thy place. Assure thee,
If I do vow a friendship, I'll perform it
To the last article. My lord shall never rest.
I'll watch him tame and talk him out of patience;
His bed shall seem a school, his board a shrift;
I'll intermingle everything he does
With Cassio's suit. Therefore be merry, Cassio,
For thy solicitor shall rather die
Than give thy cause away.

   Enter Othello and Iago

EMILIA

Madam, here comes my lord.

CASSIO

30   Madam, I'll take my leave.

DESDEMONA

Why, stay and hear me speak.

CASSIO

Madam, not now: I am very ill at ease,
Unfit for mine own purposes.

DESDEMONA

Well, do your discretion.   *Exit Cassio*

IAGO

Ha! I like not that.

OTHELLO   What dost thou say?

IAGO

Nothing, my lord; or if – I know not what.

OTHELLO

Was not that Cassio parted from my wife?

IAGO

Cassio, my lord? No, sure, I cannot think it
That he would sneak away so guilty-like,
Seeing you coming.

OTHELLO   I do believe 'twas he.   40

DESDEMONA

How now, my lord?
I have been talking with a suitor here,
A man that languishes in your displeasure.

OTHELLO

Who is't you mean?

DESDEMONA

Why, your Lieutenant, Cassio. Good my lord,
If I have any grace or power to move you,
His present reconciliation take.
For if he be not one that truly loves you,
That errs in ignorance, and not in cunning,
I have no judgement in an honest face.   50
I prithee call him back.

OTHELLO   Went he hence now?

DESDEMONA

Yes, faith; so humbled
That he hath left part of his grief with me
To suffer with him. Good love, call him back.

OTHELLO

Not now, sweet Desdemon; some other time.

DESDEMONA

But shall't be shortly?

OTHELLO   The sooner, sweet, for you.

DESDEMONA

Shall't be tonight, at supper?

OTHELLO   No, not tonight.

III.3

DESDEMONA
  Tomorrow dinner then?

OTHELLO   I shall not dine at home.
  I meet the captains at the citadel.

DESDEMONA
60 Why, then, tomorrow night, or Tuesday morn,
  On Tuesday noon, or night; on Wednesday morn.
  I prithee name the time, but let it not
  Exceed three days. In faith, he's penitent:
  And yet his trespass in our common reason –
  Save that, they say, the wars must make example
  Out of their best – is not almost a fault
  T'incur a private check. When shall he come?
  Tell me, Othello. I wonder in my soul
  What you would ask me that I should deny,
70 Or stand so mammering on? What! Michael Cassio,
  That came a-wooing with you? And so many a time –
  When I have spoke of you dispraisingly –
  Hath ta'en your part, to have so much to do
  To bring him in? By'r Lady, I could do much.

OTHELLO
  Prithee, no more: let him come when he will;
  I will deny thee nothing.

DESDEMONA   Why, this is not a boon:
  'Tis as I should entreat you wear your gloves
  Or feed on nourishing dishes, or keep you warm,
  Or sue to you to do a peculiar profit
80 To your own person. Nay, when I have a suit
  Wherein I mean to touch your love indeed
  It shall be full of poise and difficult weight,
  And fearful to be granted.

OTHELLO   I will deny thee nothing.
  Whereon, I do beseech thee, grant me this:
  To leave me but a little to my self.

I'm not asking very much.

106

DESDEMONA

Shall I deny you? No; farewell, my lord.

OTHELLO

Farewell, my Desdemona, I'll come to thee straight.

DESDEMONA

Emilia, come. Be as your fancies teach you.
Whate'er you be, I am obedient.   *essential truth.*

Exeunt Desdemona and Emilia

OTHELLO   *All is settled but*

Excellent wretch! Perdition catch my soul   90
But I do love thee! And when I love thee not,   *1. Dramatic*
Chaos is come again.   *irony*

IAGO   My noble lord –

OTHELLO   *Iago has been*

What dost thou say, Iago?   *present throughout the*

IAGO   Did Michael Cassio,   *pleading of*
When you wooed my lady, know of your love?   *Desdemona*

OTHELLO

He did, from first to last. Why dost thou ask?

IAGO

But for a satisfaction of my thought –
No further harm.

OTHELLO   Why of thy thought, Iago?

IAGO

I did not think he had been acquainted with her.

OTHELLO

O yes, and went between us very oft.

IAGO

Indeed!   100

OTHELLO

Indeed? Ay, indeed. Discern'st thou aught in that?
Is he not honest?

IAGO   Honest, my lord?

OTHELLO   Honest? Ay, honest.

IAGO

My lord, for aught I know.

OTHELLO   What dost thou think?

IAGO

Think, my lord?

OTHELLO

Think, my lord! By heaven, he echoes me,
As if there were some monster in his thought
Too hideous to be shown. Thou dost mean something.
I heard thee say even now, thou lik'st not that,
When Cassio left my wife. What didst not like?
And when I told thee he was of my counsel
In my whole course of wooing, thou cried'st 'Indeed!'
And didst contract and purse thy brow together,
As if thou then hadst shut up in thy brain
Some horrible conceit. If thou dost love me,
Show me thy thought.

IAGO

My lord, you know I love you.

OTHELLO   I think thou dost:
And for I know thou'rt full of love and honesty,
And weigh'st thy words before thou giv'st them breath,
Therefore these stops of thine affright me more:
For such things in a false disloyal knave
Are tricks of custom; but in a man that's just,
They're close dilations, working from the heart,
That passion cannot rule.

IAGO   For Michael Cassio,
I dare be sworn I think that he is honest.

OTHELLO

I think so too.

IAGO   Men should be what they seem;
Or those that be not, would they might seem none!

108

OTHELLO

Certain, men should be what they seem.

IAGO

Why, then, I think Cassio's an honest man.

OTHELLO

Nay, yet there's more in this.
I prithee speak to me as to thy thinkings,   130
As thou dost ruminate, and give thy worst of thoughts
The worst of words.

IAGO   Good my lord, pardon me;
Though I am bound to every act of duty,
I am not bound to that all slaves are free to:
Utter my thoughts. Why, say they are vile and false?
As where's that palace whereinto foul things
Sometimes intrude not? Who has a breast so pure,
But some uncleanly apprehensions
Keep leets and law-days, and in session sit
With meditations lawful?   140

OTHELLO   _O_

Thou dost conspire against thy friend, Iago,
If thou but think'st him wronged, and mak'st his ear
A stranger to thy thoughts.

IAGO   I do beseech you,
Though I perchance am vicious in my guess –
As I confess it is my nature's plague
To spy into abuses, and of my jealousy _Suspicious nature._
Shapes faults that are not – that your wisdom then,
From one that so imperfectly conjects,
Would take no notice, nor build yourself a trouble
Out of his scattering and unsure observance.   150
It were not for your quiet nor your good,
Nor for my manhood, honesty, and wisdom,
To let you know my thoughts.

OTHELLO   What dost thou mean?

IAGO

Good name in man and woman, dear my lord,
Is the immediate jewel of their souls.
Who steals my purse, steals trash; 'tis something,
        nothing;
'Twas mine, 'tis his, and has been slave to thousands:
But he that filches from me my good name
Robs me of that which not enriches him
160   And makes me poor indeed.

OTHELLO   By heaven, I'll know thy thoughts.

IAGO

You cannot, if my heart were in your hand,
Nor shall not, whilst 'tis in my custody.

OTHELLO

Ha!

IAGO   O, beware, my lord, of jealousy!
It is the green-eyed monster, which doth mock
The meat it feeds on. That cuckold lives in bliss
Who certain of his fate loves not his wronger,
But O, what damnèd minutes tells he o'er,
Who dotes yet doubts, suspects yet fondly loves!

OTHELLO

O misery!

IAGO

170   Poor and content is rich, and rich enough;
But riches fineless is as poor as winter,
To him that ever fears he shall be poor.
Good God, the souls of all my tribe defend
From jealousy!

OTHELLO   Why, why is this?
Think'st thou I'd make a life of jealousy,
To follow still the changes of the moon

With fresh suspicions? No, to be once in doubt
Is once to be resolved. Exchange me for a goat,
When I shall turn the business of my soul
To such exsufflicate and blown surmises,   180
Matching thy inference. 'Tis not to make me jealous
To say my wife is fair, loves company,
Is free of speech, sings, plays, and dances well:
Where virtue is, these are more virtuous.
Nor from mine own weak merits will I draw
The smallest fear or doubt of her revolt,
For she had eyes and chose me. No, Iago,
I'll see before I doubt; when I doubt, prove;
And on the proof, there is no more but this:
Away at once with love or jealousy! *as he does* 190

IAGO

I am glad of this: for now I shall have reason
To show the love and duty that I bear you
With franker spirit. Therefore, as I am bound,
Receive it from me. I speak not yet of proof.
Look to your wife; observe her well with Cassio.
Wear your eye thus: not jealous, nor secure.
I would not have your free and noble nature,
Out of self-bounty, be abused. Look to't.
I know our country disposition well:
In Venice they do let God see the pranks   200
They dare not show their husbands; their best
          conscience
Is not to leave't undone, but keep't unknown.

OTHELLO

Dost thou say so?

IAGO

She did deceive her father, marrying you,
And when she seemed to shake, and fear your looks,
She loved them most.

OTHELLO   And so she did.

IAGO   Why, go to, then!
She that so young could give out such a seeming,
To seel her father's eyes up close as oak –
He thought 'twas witchcraft. – But I am much to blame,
210   I humbly do beseech you of your pardon
For too much loving you.

OTHELLO   I am bound to thee for ever.

IAGO
I see this hath a little dashed your spirits.

OTHELLO
Not a jot, not a jot.

IAGO   In faith, I fear it has.
I hope you will consider what is spoke
Comes from my love. But I do see you're moved.
I am to pray you, not to strain my speech
To grosser issues, nor to larger reach
Than to suspicion.

OTHELLO
I will not.

IAGO   Should you do so, my lord,
220   My speech should fall into such vile success
Which my thoughts aimed not at. Cassio's my worthy
      friend.
My lord, I see you're moved.

OTHELLO   No, not much moved.
I do not think but Desdemona's honest.

IAGO
Long live she so! And long live you to think so!

OTHELLO
And yet, how nature erring from itself –

IAGO
Ay, there's the point: as, to be bold with you,
Not to affect many proposèd matches

Of her own clime, complexion, and degree,
Whereto we see in all things nature tends,
Foh! One may smell in such a will most rank, 230
Foul disproportion, thoughts unnatural.
But, pardon me, I do not in position
Distinctly speak of her, though I may fear
Her will, recoiling to her better judgement,
May fall to match you with her country forms,
And happily repent.

OTHELLO   Farewell, farewell.
If more thou dost perceive, let me know more.
Set on thy wife to observe. Leave me, Iago.

IAGO
(*going*) My lord, I take my leave.

OTHELLO
Why did I marry? This honest creature doubtless 240
Sees and knows more, much more than he unfolds.

IAGO
(*returning*) My lord, I would I might entreat your
                    honour
To scan this thing no farther. Leave it to time.
Although 'tis fit that Cassio have his place,
For sure he fills it up with great ability,
Yet, if you please to hold him off awhile,
You shall by that perceive him and his means;
Note if your lady strain his entertainment
With any strong or vehement importunity –
Much will be seen in that. In the meantime, 250
Let me be thought too busy in my fears,
As worthy cause I have to fear I am,
And hold her free, I do beseech your honour.

OTHELLO
Fear not my government.

IAGO   I once more take my leave. *Exit*

OTHELLO

This fellow's of exceeding honesty,
And knows all qualities with a learnèd spirit
Of human dealings. If I do prove her haggard, *wild fal...*
Though that her jesses were my dear heart-strings, *straps*
I'd whistle her off, and let her down the wind
260 To prey at fortune. Haply, for I am black
And have not those soft parts of conversation
That chamberers have; or for I am declined
Into the vale of years – yet that's not much –
She's gone: I am abused, and my relief
Must be to loathe her. O, curse of marriage!
That we can call these delicate creatures ours
And not their appetites! I had rather be a toad
And live upon the vapour of a dungeon
Than keep a corner in the thing I love
270 For others' uses. Yet 'tis the plague of great ones;
Prerogatived are they less than the base.
'Tis destiny unshunnable, like death:
Even then this forkèd plague is fated to us *cuckoldry*
When we do quicken. Desdemona comes: *from birth*
    Enter Desdemona and Emilia
If she be false, O, then heaven mocks itself!
I'll not believe't.

DESDEMONA   How now, my dear Othello!
Your dinner, and the generous islanders *noble*
By you invited, do attend your presence.

OTHELLO

I am to blame.

DESDEMONA   Why do you speak so faintly?
280 Are you not well?

OTHELLO

I have a pain upon my forehead here.

DESDEMONA

Faith, that's with watching: 'twill away again.
Let me but bind it hard, within this hour
It will be well.

OTHELLO　　　　　Your napkin is too little. ✓

He puts the handkerchief from him, and she drops it
Let it alone. Come, I'll go in with you.

DESDEMONA

I am very sorry that you are not well.

　　　　　　　　　Exeunt Othello and Desdemona

EMILIA

I am glad I have found this napkin:
This was her first remembrance from the Moor.
My wayward husband hath a hundred times
Wooed me to steal it; but she so loves the token –　　290
For he conjured her she should ever keep it –
That she reserves it evermore about her
To kiss and talk to. I'll have the work ta'en out, *copied*
And give't Iago.
What he will do with it, heaven knows, not I:
I nothing, but to please his fantasy. *manipulated by Iago*
　　　Enter Iago　　　　　　　　*as is everybody*

IAGO

How now? What do you here alone?

EMILIA

Do not you chide: I have a thing for you.

IAGO

A thing for me? It is a common thing. *her genitals*

EMILIA

Ha!　　　　　　　　　　　　　　　　　　　300

IAGO

To have a foolish wife.

EMILIA

O, is that all? What will you give me now

115

For that same handkerchief?

IAGO   What handkerchief?

EMILIA

What handkerchief!
Why that the Moor first gave to Desdemona;
That which so often you did bid me steal.

IAGO

Hast stol'n it from her?

EMILIA

No, faith, she let it drop by negligence,
And to th'advantage, I, being here, took't up.

310   Look, here it is.

IAGO   A good wench! Give it me.

EMILIA

What will you do with't, that you have been so earnest
To have me filch it?

IAGO (*snatching it*)   Why, what is that to you?

EMILIA

If it be not for some purpose of import, *ance*
Give't me again. Poor lady, she'll run mad
When she shall lack it.

IAGO

Be not acknown on't: I have use for it.
Go, leave me.   *Exit Emilia*
I will in Cassio's lodging lose this napkin,
And let him find it. Trifles light as air
320   Are to the jealous confirmations strong
As proofs of holy writ. This may do something.
The Moor already changes with my poison.
Dangerous conceits are in their natures poisons,
Which at the first are scarce found to distaste,
But, with a little act upon the blood,
Burn like the mines of sulphur.

       Enter Othello

I did say so.
Look where he comes! Not poppy, nor mandragora,
Nor all the drowsy syrups of the world,
Shall ever medicine thee to that sweet sleep
Which thou owed'st yesterday.

OTHELLO   Ha, ha, false to me!   330

IAGO
Why, how now, General! No more of that.

OTHELLO
Avaunt! Be gone! Thou hast set me on the rack.
I swear 'tis better to be much abused,
Than but to know't a little.

IAGO   How now, my lord!

OTHELLO
What sense had I of her stolen hours of lust?
I saw't not, thought it not, it harmed not me.
I slept the next night well, was free and merry;
I found not Cassio's kisses on her lips.
He that is robbed, not wanting what is stolen,
Let him not know't, and he's not robbed at all.   340

IAGO
I am sorry to hear this.

OTHELLO
I had been happy if the general camp,
Pioners and all, had tasted her sweet body,
So I had nothing known. O, now, for ever
Farewell the tranquil mind! Farewell content!
Farewell the plumèd troops and the big wars
That make ambition virtue – O, farewell!
Farewell the neighing steed, and the shrill trump,
The spirit-stirring drum, th'ear-piercing fife,
The royal banner and all quality,   350
Pride, pomp and circumstance of glorious war!
And, O you mortal engines, whose rude throats

117

lost all motivation

III.3

Th'immortal Jove's dread clamours counterfeit,
Farewell! Othello's occupation's gone.

IAGO

Is't possible, my lord?

OTHELLO

Villain, be sure thou prove my love a whore;
Be sure of it: give me the ocular proof,
Or by the worth of mine eternal soul,
Modern
Thou hadst been better have been born a dog
360   Than answer my waked wrath!

IAGO   Is't come to this?

OTHELLO

Make me to see't: or, at the least, so prove it
That the probation bear no hinge nor loop
To hang a doubt on – or woe upon thy life!

IAGO

My noble lord –

OTHELLO

If thou dost slander her and torture me,
Never pray more; abandon all remorse;
On horror's head horrors accumulate;
Do deeds to make heaven weep, all earth amazed:
For nothing canst thou to damnation add
370   Greater than that.

IAGO   O grace! O heaven defend me!
Are you a man? Have you a soul? Or sense?
God bu'y you: take mine office. O wretched fool,
That lov'st to make thine honesty a vice!
O monstrous world! Take note, take note, O world!
To be direct and honest is not safe.
I thank you for this profit, and from hence
I'll love no friend, sith love breeds such offence.

OTHELLO

Nay, stay: thou shouldst be honest.

118

IAGO

I should be wise; for honesty's a fool
And loses that it works for.

OTHELLO   By the world,

380

I think my wife be honest, and think she is not;
I think that thou art just, and think thou art not.
I'll have some proof. Her name that was as fresh
As Dian's visage is now begrimed and black
As mine own face. If there be cords or knives,
Poison or fire or suffocating streams,
I'll not endure it. Would I were satisfied!

IAGO

I see, sir, you are eaten up with passion.
I do repent me that I put it to you.
You would be satisfied?

OTHELLO   Would! Nay, I will.

390

IAGO

And may. But how? How satisfied, my lord?
Would you, the supervisor, grossly gape on?
Behold her topped?

OTHELLO   Death and damnation! O!

IAGO

It were a tedious difficulty, I think,
To bring them to that prospect. Damn them then
If ever mortal eyes do see them bolster
More than their own! What then? How then?
What shall I say? Where's satisfaction?
It is impossible you should see this,
Were they as prime as goats, as hot as monkeys,

400

As salt as wolves in pride, and fools as gross
As ignorance made drunk. But yet, I say,
If imputation and strong circumstance,
Which lead directly to the door of truth,
Will give you satisfaction, you might have't.

119

OTHELLO

Give me a living reason she's disloyal.

IAGO

I do not like the office.

But sith I am entered in this cause so far –

Pricked to't by foolish honesty and love –

410 I will go on. I lay with Cassio lately,

And being troubled with a raging tooth

I could not sleep.

There are a kind of men so loose of soul

That in their sleeps will mutter their affairs:

One of this kind is Cassio.

In sleep I heard him say: 'Sweet Desdemona,

Let us be wary, let us hide our loves';

And then, sir, would he gripe and wring my hand,

Cry 'O sweet creature!' and then kiss me hard,

420 As if he plucked up kisses by the roots,

That grew upon my lips; then laid his leg

Over my thigh, and sighed and kissed, and then

Cried 'Cursèd fate that gave thee to the Moor!'

OTHELLO

O monstrous! Monstrous!

IAGO   Nay, this was but his dream.

OTHELLO

But this denoted a foregone conclusion.

IAGO

'Tis a shrewd doubt, though it be but a dream:

And this may help to thicken other proofs

That do demonstrate thinly.

OTHELLO   I'll tear her all to pieces!

IAGO

Nay, but be wise: yet we see nothing done,

430 She may be honest yet. Tell me but this:

Have you not sometimes seen a handkerchief,

Spotted with strawberries, in your wife's hand?

OTHELLO

I gave her such a one: 'twas my first gift.

IAGO

I know not that: but such a handkerchief –
I am sure it was your wife's – did I today
See Cassio wipe his beard with.

OTHELLO   If it be that –

IAGO

If it be that, or any that was hers,
It speaks against her with the other proofs.

OTHELLO

O, that the slave had forty thousand lives!
One is too poor, too weak for my revenge.   440
Now do I see 'tis true. Look here, Iago –
All my fond love thus do I blow to heaven:
'Tis gone.
Arise, black vengeance, from thy hollow cell!
Yield up, O love, thy crown and hearted throne
To tyrannous hate! Swell, bosom, with thy fraught,
For 'tis of aspics' tongues!

IAGO   Yet be content.

OTHELLO

O, blood, blood, blood!

IAGO

Patience, I say: your mind perhaps may change.

OTHELLO

Never, Iago. Like to the Pontic sea, *Black Sea*   450
Whose icy current and compulsive course
Ne'er feels retiring ebb, but keeps due on
To the Propontic and the Hellespont, *Dardanelles*
Even so my bloody thoughts with violent pace
Shall ne'er look back, ne'er ebb to humble love,
Till that a capable and wide revenge

Swallow them up. Now, by yond marble heaven,
In the due reverence of a sacred vow
I here engage my words.
> *He kneels*

IAGO   Do not rise yet.
> *He kneels*

460 Witness you ever-burning lights above,
You elements, that clip us round about,
Witness that here Iago doth give up
The execution of his wit, hands, heart,
To wronged Othello's service. Let him command,
And to obey shall be in me remorse,
What bloody business ever.
> *They rise*

OTHELLO   I greet thy love,
Not with vain thanks, but with acceptance bounteous;
And will upon the instant put thee to't.
Within these three days let me hear thee say
470 That Cassio's not alive.

IAGO   My friend is dead;
'Tis done at your request. But let her live.

OTHELLO
Damn her, lewd minx! O, damn her, damn her!
Come go with me apart. I will withdraw
To furnish me with some swift means of death
For the fair devil. Now art thou my Lieutenant.

IAGO
I am your own for ever.   *Exeunt*

III.4   *Enter Desdemona, Emilia, and Clown*

DESDEMONA Do you know, sirrah, where Lieutenant
Cassio lies?

CLOWN I dare not say he lies anywhere.

122

DESDEMONA Why, man?

CLOWN He's a soldier, and for one to say a soldier lies is
stabbing.

DESDEMONA Go to! Where lodges he?

CLOWN To tell you where he lodges is to tell you where I
lie.

DESDEMONA Can anything be made of this?   10

CLOWN I know not where he lodges, and for me to devise a
lodging, and say he lies here, or he lies there, were to lie
in mine own throat.

DESDEMONA Can you inquire him out? And be edified by
report?

CLOWN I will catechize the world for him, that is, make
questions, and by them answer.

DESDEMONA Seek him; bid him come hither; tell him I
have moved my lord on his behalf, and hope all will be
well.   20

CLOWN To do this is within the compass of man's wit, and
therefore I will attempt the doing of it.   *Exit*

DESDEMONA
Where should I lose that handkerchief, Emilia?

EMILIA
I know not, madam.

DESDEMONA
Believe me, I had rather have lost my purse
Full of crusadoes; and, but my noble Moor
Is true of mind, and made of no such baseness
As jealous creatures are, it were enough
To put him to ill-thinking.

EMILIA   Is he not jealous?

DESDEMONA
Who? He? I think the sun where he was born   30
Drew all such humours from him.

EMILIA   Look where he comes.

123

Enter Othello

DESDEMONA

    I will not leave him now till Cassio

    Be called to him. How is't with you, my lord?

OTHELLO

    Well, my good lady. (*Aside*) O, hardness to dissemble!

    How do you, Desdemona?

DESDEMONA   Well, my good lord.

OTHELLO

    Give me your hand. This hand is moist, my lady.

DESDEMONA

    It yet has felt no age, nor known no sorrow.

OTHELLO

    This argues fruitfulness and liberal heart.

    Hot, hot and moist. This hand of yours requires

40   A sequester from liberty, fasting and prayer,

    Much castigation, exercise devout;

    For there's a young and sweating devil here

    That commonly rebels. 'Tis a good hand,

    A frank one.

DESDEMONA   You may, indeed, say so:

    For 'twas that hand that gave away my heart.

OTHELLO

    A liberal hand! The hearts of old gave hands;

    But our new heraldry is hands, not hearts.

DESDEMONA

    I cannot speak of this. Come now, your promise.

OTHELLO

    What promise, chuck?

DESDEMONA

50   I have sent to bid Cassio come speak with you.

OTHELLO

    I have a salt and sorry rheum offends me:

    Lend me thy handkerchief.

DESDEMONA   Here, my lord.

OTHELLO
  That which I gave you.

DESDEMONA   I have it not about me.

OTHELLO
  Not?

DESDEMONA   No, faith, my lord.

OTHELLO   That is a fault.
  That handkerchief
  Did an Egyptian to my mother give:
  She was a charmer and could almost read
  The thoughts of people. She told her, while she kept it,
  'Twould make her amiable and subdue my father
  Entirely to her love; but, if she lost it   60
  Or made a gift of it, my father's eye
  Should hold her loathèd, and his spirits should hunt
  After new fancies. She, dying, gave it me,
  And bid me, when my fate would have me wive,
  To give it her. I did so; and take heed on't:
  Make it a darling, like your precious eye.
  To lose or give't away were such perdition
  As nothing else could match.

DESDEMONA   Is't possible?

OTHELLO
  'Tis true: there's magic in the web of it.
  A sibyl, that had numbered in the world   70
  The sun to course two hundred compasses,
  In her prophetic fury sewed the work:
  The worms were hallowed that did breed the silk,
  And it was dyed in mummy, which the skilful
  Conserved of maidens' hearts.

DESDEMONA   Indeed! Is't true?

OTHELLO
  Most veritable; therefore look to't well.

125

III.4

DESDEMONA
Then would to God that I had never seen it!

OTHELLO
Ha! Wherefore?

DESDEMONA
Why do you speak so startingly and rash?

OTHELLO
80   Is't lost? Is't gone? Speak: is't out o'th'way?

DESDEMONA
Heaven bless us!

OTHELLO   Say you?

DESDEMONA   It is not lost.
But what an if it were?

OTHELLO   How!

DESDEMONA
I say it is not lost.

OTHELLO   Fetch't: let me see't.

DESDEMONA
Why, so I can, sir; but I will not now.
This is a trick to put me from my suit.
Pray you let Cassio be received again.

OTHELLO
Fetch me the handkerchief: my mind misgives.

DESDEMONA
Come, come:
You'll never meet a more sufficient man.

OTHELLO
90   The handkerchief!

DESDEMONA   I pray, talk me of Cassio.

OTHELLO
The handkerchief!

DESDEMONA   A man that all his time
Hath founded his good fortunes on your love;
Shared dangers with you –

126

OTHELLO
　The handkerchief!

DESDEMONA　　　　I'faith you are to blame.

OTHELLO
　Zounds!

Exit cannot contain himself

EMILIA
　Is not this man jealous?

DESDEMONA　　　　I ne'er saw this before.
　Sure, there's some wonder in this handkerchief:
　I am most unhappy in the loss of it.

EMILIA
　'Tis not a year or two shows us a man.
　They are all but stomachs, and we all but food;　　100
　They eat us hungerly, and when they are full,
　They belch us. Look you, Cassio and my husband.
　　　Enter Iago and Cassio

IAGO
　There is no other way: 'tis she must do't.
　And lo, the happiness! Go, and importune her.

DESDEMONA
　How now, good Cassio! What's the news with you?

CASSIO
　Madam, my former suit. I do beseech you
　That by your virtuous means I may again
　Exist and be a member of his love,
　Whom I, with all the office of my heart,
　Entirely honour. I would not be delayed.　　110
　If my offence be of such mortal kind
　That nor my service past, nor present sorrow,
　Nor purposed merit in futurity,
　Can ransom me into his love again,
　But to know so must be my benefit:
　So shall I clothe me in a forced content,
　And shut myself up in some other course

To Fortune's alms.

DESDEMONA   Alas, thrice-gentle Cassio!
My advocation is not now in tune:
120 My lord is not my lord; nor should I know him,
Were he in favour as in humour altered.
So help me every spirit sanctified
As I have spoken for you all my best,
And stood within the blank of his displeasure
For my free speech! You must awhile be patient.
What I can do, I will; and more I will,
Than for myself I dare. Let that suffice you.

IAGO
Is my lord angry?

EMILIA   He went hence but now
And certainly in strange unquietness.

IAGO
130 Can he be angry? I have seen the cannon
When it hath blown his ranks into the air,
And like the devil from his very arm
Puffed his own brother – and can he be angry?
Something of moment then. I will go meet him.
There's matter in't indeed if he be angry.

DESDEMONA
I prithee do so.   *Exit Iago*
          Something, sure, of state,
Either from Venice, or some unhatched practice
Made demonstrable here in Cyprus to him,
Hath puddled his clear spirit; and in such cases
140 Men's natures wrangle with inferior things,
Though great ones are their object. 'Tis even so.
For let our finger ache, and it endues
Our healthful members even to that sense
Of pain. Nay, we must think men are not gods,
Nor of them look for such observancy

As fits the bridal. Beshrew me much, Emilia,
I was – unhandsome warrior as I am –
Arraigning his unkindness with my soul;
But now I find I had suborned the witness
And he's indicted falsely.   150

EMILIA

Pray heaven it be state matters, as you think,
And no conception nor no jealous toy
Concerning you.

DESDEMONA

Alas the day, I never gave him cause.

EMILIA

But jealous souls will not be answered so;
They are not ever jealous for the cause,
But jealous for they're jealous. It is a monster
Begot upon itself, born on itself.

DESDEMONA

Heaven keep that monster from Othello's mind.

EMILIA

Lady, amen!   160

DESDEMONA

I will go seek him. Cassio, walk here about.
If I do find him fit, I'll move your suit,
And seek to effect it to my uttermost.

CASSIO

I humbly thank your ladyship.

                              Exeunt Desdemona and Emilia
        Enter Bianca

BIANCA

'Save you, friend Cassio.

CASSIO   What make you from home?
How is it with you, my most fair Bianca?
I'faith, sweet love, I was coming to your house.

                              129

BIANCA

And I was going to your lodging, Cassio.
What! Keep a week away? Seven days and nights?
Eight score eight hours? And lovers' absent hours
More tedious than the dial eight score times!
O weary reckoning!

CASSIO   Pardon me, Bianca.

I have this while with leaden thoughts been pressed:
But I shall in a more continuate time
Strike off this score of absence. Sweet Bianca,
Take me this work out.

BIANCA   O Cassio, whence came this?

This is some token from a newer friend.
To the felt absence now I feel a cause.
Is't come to this? Well, well.

CASSIO   Go to, woman!

Throw your vile guesses in the devil's teeth
From whence you have them. You are jealous now
That this is from some mistress, some remembrance:
No, by my faith, Bianca.

BIANCA   Why, whose is it?

CASSIO

I know not, sweet. I found it in my chamber.
I like the work well. Ere it be demanded –
As like enough it will – I'd have it copied.
Take it and do't, and leave me for this time.

BIANCA

Leave you? Wherefore?

CASSIO

I do attend here on the General,
And think it no addition, nor my wish,
To have him see me womaned.

BIANCA   Why, I pray you?

130

CASSIO

  Not that I love you not.

BIANCA   But that you do not love me.

  I pray you, bring me on the way a little,

  And say if I shall see you soon at night.

CASSIO

  'Tis but a little way that I can bring you,

  For I attend here: but I'll see you soon.

BIANCA

  'Tis very good: I must be circumstanced.   *Exeunt*

*

Enter Othello and Iago   IV.1

IAGO

  Will you think so?

OTHELLO   Think so, Iago?

IAGO   What!

  To kiss in private?

OTHELLO   An unauthorized kiss.

IAGO

  Or to be naked with her friend in bed

  An hour or more, not meaning any harm?

OTHELLO

  Naked in bed, Iago, and not mean harm?

  It is hypocrisy against the devil.

  They that mean virtuously and yet do so,

  The devil their virtue tempts, and they tempt heaven.

IAGO

  So they do nothing, 'tis a venial slip.

  But if I give my wife a handkerchief –   10

OTHELLO

  What then?

131

IV.1

IAGO

Why, then, 'tis hers, my lord, and being hers,
She may, I think, bestow't on any man.

OTHELLO

She is protectress of her honour too.
May she give that?

IAGO

Her honour is an essence that's not seen:
They have it very oft that have it not.
But for the handkerchief –

OTHELLO

By heaven, I would most gladly have forgot it!
Thou said'st – O, it comes o'er my memory
As doth the raven o'er the infected house, *Cassio:*
Boding to all! – he had my handkerchief. *(Iago has said so)*

IAGO

Ay, what of that?

OTHELLO   That's not so good now.

IAGO   *What*

If I had said, I had seen him do you wrong, *Cassio*
Or heard him say – as knaves be such abroad,
Who having by their own importunate suit
Or voluntary dotage of some mistress
Convincèd or supplied them, cannot choose *Overcome or satisfied*
But they must blab –

OTHELLO   Hath he said anything?

IAGO

He hath, my lord; but be you well assured,
No more than he'll unswear.

OTHELLO   What hath he said?

IAGO

Faith, that he did – I know not what he did.

OTHELLO

What? What?

132

IAGO
  Lie –

OTHELLO With her?

IAGO   With her, on her, what you will.

OTHELLO Lie with her? Lie on her? We say lie on her *about*
  when they belie her. Lie with her! Zounds, that's ful-
  some! Handkerchief – confession – handkerchief! To
  confess and be hanged for his labour. First to be hanged *Confused*
  and then to confess! I tremble at it. Nature would not
  invest herself in such shadowing passion without some   40
  instruction. It is <u>not words</u> that shakes me thus! Pish!
  Noses, ears, and lips! Is't possible? – Confess? Handkerchief! O devil!
    He falls   *epileptic fit*

IAGO
  Work on,
  My medicine, work! Thus credulous fools are caught,
  And many worthy and chaste dames even thus,
  All guiltless, meet reproach. What ho, my lord!
  My lord, I say! Othello!
    Enter Cassio

               How now, Cassio!

CASSIO
  What's the matter?

IAGO
  My lord is fallen into an epilepsy.   50
  This is his second fit: he had one yesterday.

CASSIO
  Rub him about the temples.

IAGO   No, forbear.
  The lethargy must have his quiet course.
  If not, he foams at mouth; and by and by
  Breaks out to savage madness. Look, he stirs.
  Do you withdraw yourself a little while:

He will recover straight. When he is gone,
I would on great occasion speak with you.

Exit Cassio

How is it, General? Have you not hurt your head?

OTHELLO

60   Dost thou mock me?

IAGO   I mock you? No, by heaven!
Would you would bear your fortune like a man!

OTHELLO *[Cuckold]*

A hornèd man's a monster and a beast.

IAGO

The ⸻ many a beast then in a populous city,
And many a civil monster.

OTHELLO

Did he confess it?

IAGO   Good sir, be a man.
Think every bearded fellow that's but yoked *married*
[oxen] May draw with you. There's millions now alive
[oron.] That nightly lie in those unproper beds *not their own*
Which they dare swear peculiar. Your case is better.
70   O, 'tis the spite of hell, the fiend's arch-mock,
[at least you know] To lip a wanton in a secure couch,
[she's unfaithful] And to suppose her chaste! No, let me know; *I'm deceived*
And knowing what I am, I know what shall be.

OTHELLO

O, thou art wise, 'tis certain.

IAGO   Stand you awhile apart;
Confine yourself but in a patient list.
[in your fit] Whilst you were here, o'erwhelmèd with your grief –
A passion most unsuiting such a man –
Cassio came hither. I shifted him away
And laid good scuse upon your ecstasy; *[fit]*
80   Bade him anon return and here speak with me,
The which he promised. Do but encave yourself,

Sneers

And mark the fleers, the gibes, and notable scorns
That dwell in every region of his face.
For I will make him tell the tale anew,
Where, how, how oft, how long ago, and when
He hath, and is again, to cope your wife.
I say, but mark his gestures. Marry, patience! — *giving orders to O.*
Or I shall say you're all in all in spleen
And nothing of a man.

OTHELLO   Dost thou hear, Iago? *obedient.*
I will be found most cunning in my patience,   90
But – dost thou hear? – most bloody.

IAGO   That's not amiss,
But yet keep time in all. Will you withdraw? *puppet.*

                              Othello retires

Now will I question Cassio of Bianca,
A housewife, that by selling her desires
Buys herself bread and clothes. It is a creature
That dotes on Cassio – as 'tis the strumpet's plague
To beguile many and be beguiled by one.
He, when he hears of her, cannot refrain *Knowledge of character.*
From the excess of laughter. Here he comes.

     Enter Cassio

As he shall smile, Othello shall go mad;   100
And his unbookish jealousy must construe *naïve*
Poor Cassio's smiles, gestures, and light behaviour
Quite in the wrong. How do you now, Lieutenant? *Sarcasm.*

CASSIO
The worser that you give me the addition *title*
Whose want even kills me.

IAGO
Ply Desdemona well and you are sure on't.
Now if this suit lay in Bianca's power,
How quickly should you speed! *dismissive of Bianca*

CASSIO   Alas, poor caitiff! —

IV.1

OTHELLO
(*aside*) Look, how he laughs already!

IAGO
110   I never knew a woman love man so.

CASSIO
Alas, poor rogue! I think i'faith she loves me.

OTHELLO
(*aside*) Now he denies it faintly, and laughs it out.

IAGO
Do you hear, Cassio?

OTHELLO
(*aside*) Now he importunes him to tell it o'er.
Go to, well said, well said!

IAGO
She gives it out that you shall marry her.
Do you intend it?

CASSIO
Ha, ha, ha!

OTHELLO
(*aside*) Do you triumph, Roman? Do you triumph?

CASSIO I marry her! What! A customer! Prithee bear some charity to my wit: do not think it so unwholesome. Ha, ha, ha! *Give me some credit for intelligence!*

OTHELLO (*aside*) So, so, so, so: they laugh that win.

IAGO Faith, the cry goes that you shall marry her.

CASSIO Prithee, say true.

IAGO I am a very villain else.

OTHELLO (*aside*) Have you scored me? Well.

CASSIO This is the monkey's own giving out. She is persuaded I will marry her out of her own love and
130   flattery, not out of my promise.

OTHELLO (*aside*) Iago beckons me. Now he begins the story.

CASSIO She was here even now. She haunts me in every

136

*and sees handkerchief; hears Bianca
say Cassio gave it to her.*

place. I was the other day talking on the sea-bank with
certain Venetians, and thither comes the bauble and, by
this hand, falls me thus about my neck.

OTHELLO (*aside*) Crying 'O dear Cassio!' as it were. His
gesture imports it.

CASSIO So hangs and lolls and weeps upon me, so hales
and pulls me. Ha, ha, ha!   140

OTHELLO (*aside*) Now he tells how she plucked him to
my chamber. O, I see that nose of yours, but not that
dog I shall throw it to!

CASSIO Well, I must leave her company.

IAGO Before me! Look where she comes.   *strumpet*

CASSIO 'Tis such another fitchew! Marry, a perfumed one!

        Enter Bianca

What do you mean by this haunting of me?

BIANCA Let the devil and his dam haunt you! What did
you mean by that same handkerchief you gave me even
now? I was a fine fool to take it. I must take out the 150
work! A likely piece of work, that you should find it in
your chamber, and not know who left it there! This is
some minx's token, and I must take out the work?
There, give it your hobby-horse, wheresoever you had
it. I'll take out no work on't.

CASSIO How now, my sweet Bianca! How now, how now!

OTHELLO (*aside*) By heaven, that should be my handkerchief!

BIANCA If you'll come to supper tonight, you may. If you
will not, come when you are next prepared for.   *Exit* 160

IAGO After her, after her!

CASSIO Faith I must: she'll rail in the street else.

IAGO Will you sup there?

CASSIO Faith, I intend to.

IAGO Well, I may chance to see you: for I would very fain
speak with you.

IV.1

CASSIO Prithee come, will you?

IAGO Go to! Say no more.   *Exit Cassio*

OTHELLO (*coming forward*) How shall I murder him, Iago?

170 IAGO Did you perceive how he laughed at his vice?

OTHELLO O, Iago!

IAGO And did you see the handkerchief?

OTHELLO Was that mine?

IAGO Yours, by this hand! And to see how he prizes the foolish woman your wife: she gave it him, and he hath giv'n it his whore.

OTHELLO I would have him nine years a-killing! – A fine woman, a fair woman, a sweet woman!

IAGO Nay, you must forget that.

180 OTHELLO Ay, let her rot and perish, and be damned tonight, for she shall not live! No, my heart is turned to stone: I strike it, and it hurts my hand. – O, the world hath not a sweeter creature! She might lie by an emperor's side and command him tasks.

IAGO Nay, that's not your way.

no matter nowadays

OTHELLO Hang her! I do but say what she is: so delicate with her needle, an admirable musician! O, she will sing the savageness out of a bear! Of so high and plenteous wit and invention!

190 IAGO She's the worse for all this.

OTHELLO O, a thousand, thousand times! – And then of so gentle a condition.

IAGO Ay, too gentle.

OTHELLO Nay, that's certain – but yet the pity of it, Iago! O, Iago, the pity of it, Iago!

foolish letter seton with it

IAGO If you are so fond over her iniquity, give her patent to offend, for if it touch not you, it comes near nobody.   *no one else cares*

OTHELLO I will chop her into messes! Cuckold me!

200 IAGO O, 'tis foul in her!

138

OTHELLO With mine officer!

IAGO That's fouler.

OTHELLO Get me some poison, Iago, this night. I'll not
expostulate with her, lest her body and beauty unprovide
my mind again – this night, Iago.

IAGO Do it not with poison; strangle her in her bed, even
the bed she hath contaminated.

OTHELLO Good, good! The justice of it pleases; very
good!

IAGO And for Cassio, let me be his undertaker. You shall 210
hear more by midnight.

OTHELLO

Excellent good!

Trumpet sounds

What trumpet is that same?

IAGO

I warrant, something from Venice.

Enter Lodovico, Desdemona, and attendants

'Tis Lodovico,

Come from the Duke; and see your wife is with him.

LODOVICO

God save you, worthy General!

OTHELLO   With all my heart, sir.

LODOVICO

The Duke and Senators of Venice greet you.

He gives him a letter

OTHELLO

I kiss the instrument of their pleasures.

He reads the letter

DESDEMONA

And what's the news, good cousin Lodovico?

IAGO

I am very glad to see you, signor:

Welcome to Cyprus.   220

LODOVICO

I thank you. How does Lieutenant Cassio?

IAGO

Lives, sir.

DESDEMONA

Cousin, there's fallen between him and my lord
An unkind breach; but you shall make all well.

OTHELLO

Are you sure of that?

DESDEMONA

My lord?

OTHELLO

'This fail you not to do, as you will' –

LODOVICO

He did not call: he's busy in the paper.
Is there division 'twixt my lord and Cassio?

DESDEMONA

230   A most unhappy one; I would do much
T'atone them, for the love I bear to Cassio.

OTHELLO

Fire and brimstone!

DESDEMONA

My lord?

OTHELLO

Are you wise?

DESDEMONA

What, is he angry?

LODOVICO   Maybe the letter moved him.

For, as I think, they do command him home,
Deputing Cassio in his government.

DESDEMONA

By my troth, I am glad on't.

OTHELLO   Indeed!

DESDEMONA   My lord?

OTHELLO

I am glad to see you mad.

DESDEMONA   Why, sweet Othello!

OTHELLO

Devil!   240

He strikes her

DESDEMONA

I have not deserved this.

LODOVICO

My lord, this would not be believed in Venice,

Though I should swear I saw't. 'Tis very much.

Make her amends; she weeps.

OTHELLO   O devil, devil!

If that the earth could teem with woman's tears,

Each drop she falls would prove a crocodile.   *Falte*

Out of my sight!

DESDEMONA   I will not stay to offend you.

LODOVICO

Truly an obedient lady.

I do beseech your lordship call her back.

OTHELLO

Mistress!   250

DESDEMONA

My lord?

OTHELLO

What would you with her, sir?

LODOVICO

Who? I, my lord?

OTHELLO

Ay, you did wish that I would make her turn.

Sir, she can turn, and turn, and yet go on,

And turn again. And she can weep, sir, weep.

And she's obedient; as you say, obedient,

Very obedient – proceed you in your tears –

Concerning this, sir – O, well-painted passion! –
260 I am commanded home – get you away!
I'll send for you anon. – Sir, I obey the mandate,
And will return to Venice. – Hence, avaunt!

Exit Desdemona

Cassio shall have my place. And sir, tonight
I do entreat that we may sup together.
You are welcome, sir, to Cyprus. Goats and monkeys!

Symbols of lust. *Exit*

LODOVICO
Is this the noble Moor, whom our full senate
Call all-in-all sufficient? Is this the nature
Whom passion could not shake? Whose solid virtue
The shot of accident nor dart of chance
270 Could neither graze nor pierce?

IAGO   He is much changed.

LODOVICO
Are his wits safe? Is he not light of brain?

IAGO
He's that he is: I may not breathe my censure
What he might be. If what he might he is not,
I would to heaven he were.

LODOVICO   What! Strike his wife!

IAGO
Faith, that was not so well: yet would I knew
That stroke would prove the worst!

LODOVICO   Is it his use?
Or did the letters work upon his blood
And new-create this fault?

IAGO   Alas, alas!
It is not honesty in me to speak
280 What I have seen and known. You shall observe him,
And his own courses will denote him so,
That I may save my speech. Do but go after,

Destructive
of O's
reputation

142

And mark how he continues.

LODOVICO
I am sorry that I am deceived in him.

Enter Othello and Emilia

OTHELLO
You have seen nothing then?

EMILIA
Nor ever heard, nor ever did suspect.

OTHELLO
Yes, you have seen Cassio and she together.

EMILIA
But then I saw no harm; and then I heard
Each syllable that breath made up between them.

OTHELLO
What! Did they never whisper?

EMILIA   Never, my lord.

OTHELLO
Nor send you out o'th'way?

EMILIA   Never.

OTHELLO
To fetch her fan, her gloves, her mask, nor nothing?

EMILIA
Never, my lord.

OTHELLO
That's strange.   10

EMILIA
I durst, my lord, to wager she is honest,
Lay down my soul at stake. If you think other,
Remove your thought: it doth abuse your bosom.
If any wretch have put this in your head,
Let heaven requite it with the serpent's curse! *on Eve*
For if she be not honest, chaste, and true,

There's no man happy. The purest of their wives
Is foul as slander.

OTHELLO   Bid her come hither: go!

Exit Emilia

She says enough; yet she's a simple bawd
20 That cannot say as much. This is a subtle whore,
A closet lock and key of villainous secrets;
And yet she'll kneel and pray – I have seen her do't.

Enter Desdemona and Emilia

DESDEMONA
My lord, what is your will?

OTHELLO   Pray, chuck, come hither.

DESDEMONA
What is your pleasure?

OTHELLO   Let me see your eyes.
Look in my face.

DESDEMONA   What horrible fancy's this?

OTHELLO (*to Emilia*)
Some of your function, mistress.
Leave procreants alone and shut the door.
Cough or cry 'hem' if anybody come.
Your mystery, your mystery! Nay, dispatch! *Exit Emilia*

DESDEMONA
30 Upon my knees, what doth your speech import?
I understand a fury in your words,
But not the words.

OTHELLO   Why, what art thou?

DESDEMONA
Your wife, my lord; your true and loyal wife.

OTHELLO
Come, swear it; damn thyself;
Lest being like one of heaven, the devils themselves
Should fear to seize thee. Therefore be double-damned:
Swear thou art honest.

DESDEMONA   Heaven doth truly know it.

144

OTHELLO

Heaven truly knows that thou art false as hell.

DESDEMONA

To whom, my lord? With whom? How am I false?

OTHELLO

Ah, Desdemon! Away, away, away! *Grief.* 40

DESDEMONA

Alas, the heavy day! Why do you weep?
Am I the motive of these tears my lord? *If you think my*
If haply you my father do suspect *father is behind your*
An instrument of this your calling back, *recall to Venice*
Lay not your blame on me. If <u>you</u> have lost him,
I have lost him too.

OTHELLO   Had it pleased heaven
To try me with affliction, had they rained
All kind of sores and shames on my bare head,
Steeped me in poverty to the very lips,
Given to captivity me and my utmost hopes, 50
I should have found in some place of my soul
A drop of patience. But alas, to make me
A fixed figure for the time of scorn
To point his slow unmoving finger at!
Yet could I bear that too, well, very well:
But there where I have garnered up my heart, *Terrible*
Where either I must live, or bear no life, *Poetry.*
The fountain from the which my current runs,
Or else dries up – to be discarded thence
Or keep it as a cistern for foul toads 60
To knot and gender in! Turn thy complexion there,
Patience, thou young and rose-lipped cherubin,
Ay, there look grim as hell!

DESDEMONA

I hope my noble lord esteems me honest.

OTHELLO

O, ay! As summer flies are in the shambles, *butcher's*
slaughter-house

anthem

That quicken even with blowing, O, thou weed,
Who art so lovely fair, and smell'st so sweet
That the sense aches at thee, would thou hadst ne'er
        been born!

DESDEMONA

Alas, what ignorant sin have I committed?

OTHELLO

70   Was this fair paper, this most goodly book,
Made to write 'whore' upon? What committed!
Committed? O, thou public commoner!
I should make very forges of my cheeks,
That would to cinders burn up modesty,
Did I but speak thy deeds. What committed?
Heaven stops the nose at it, and the moon winks;
The bawdy wind, that kisses all it meets,
Is hushed within the hollow mine of earth
And will not hear it. What committed?
Impudent strumpet!

trimble poetry (so much of this speech)

80   DESDEMONA   By heaven, you do me wrong.

OTHELLO

Are you not a strumpet?

DESDEMONA   No, as I am a Christian.

If to preserve this vessel for my lord
From any other foul unlawful touch,
Be not to be a strumpet, I am none.

OTHELLO

What! Not a whore?

DESDEMONA   No, as I shall be saved.

OTHELLO

Is't possible?

DESDEMONA

O, heaven forgive us!

OTHELLO   I cry you mercy then:

I took you for that cunning whore of Venice

146

That married with Othello. (*Calling*) You, mistress,
That have the office opposite to Saint Peter   90
And keep the gate of hell!   *Pain*

> *Enter Emilia*

                              You, you, ay, you!   *insulting*
                                                   as to procuress
We have done our course: there's money for your pains.
I pray you turn the key, and keep our counsel.   *Exit*

EMILIA
  Alas, what does this gentleman conceive?
  How do you, madam? How do you, my good lady?

DESDEMONA
  Faith, half asleep.

EMILIA
  Good madam, what's the matter with my lord?

DESDEMONA
  With who?

EMILIA
  Why, with my lord, madam.

DESDEMONA
  Who is thy lord?

EMILIA   He that is yours, sweet lady.   100

DESDEMONA
  I have none. Do not talk to me, Emilia:
  I cannot weep; nor answers have I none,
  But what should go by water. Prithee tonight
  Lay on my bed my wedding sheets, remember,
  And call thy husband hither

EMILIA   Here's a change indeed!
                                                   Exit

DESDEMONA
  'Tis meet I should be used so, very meet.   *accepts his*
  How have I been behaved, that he might stick   *right to*
                                                  criticise her for
  The smallest opinion on my least misuse?   *her slightest faults*

> *Enter Emilia and Iago*

IAGO

What is your pleasure, madam? How is't with you?

DESDEMONA

110   I cannot tell: those that do teach young babes
Do it with gentle means and easy tasks:
He might have chid me so, for, in good faith,
I am a child to chiding.

IAGO   What is the matter, lady?

EMILIA

Alas, Iago, my lord hath so bewhored her,
Thrown such despite and heavy terms upon her
As true heart cannot bear.

DESDEMONA

Am I that name, Iago?

IAGO   What name, fair lady?

DESDEMONA

Such as she said my lord did say I was.

EMILIA

He called her whore: a beggar in his drink
120   Could not have laid such terms upon his callet.

IAGO

Why did he so?

DESDEMONA

I do not know: I am sure I am none such.

IAGO

Do not weep, do not weep. Alas the day!

EMILIA

Hath she forsook so many noble matches,
Her father, and her country, all her friends,
To be called whore? Would it not make one weep?

DESDEMONA

It is my wretched fortune.

IAGO   Beshrew him for't!
How comes this trick upon him?

DESDEMONA   Nay, heaven doth know.

EMILIA

I will be hanged if some eternal villain,
Some busy and insinuating rogue,   130
Some cogging, cozening slave, to get some office,
Have not devised this slander; I'll be hanged else.

IAGO

Fie, there is no such man! It is impossible.

DESDEMONA

If any such there be, heaven pardon him.

EMILIA

A halter pardon him and hell gnaw his bones!
Why should he call her whore? Who keeps her company?
What place, what time, what form, what likelihood?
The Moor's abused by some most villainous knave,
Some base notorious knave, some scurvy fellow.
O heaven, that such companions thou'dst unfold,   140
And put in every honest hand a whip
To lash the rascals naked through the world,
Even from the east to th'west!

IAGO   Speak within door.

EMILIA

O fie upon them! Some such squire he was
That turned your wit the seamy side without
And made you to suspect _me_ with the Moor.

IAGO

You are a fool, go to.

DESDEMONA   O good Iago,
What shall I do to win my lord again?
Good friend, go to him; for, by this light of heaven,
I know not how I lost him. Here I kneel: 150
If e'er my will did trespass 'gainst his love,
Either in discourse of thought or actual deed;
Or that mine eyes, mine ears, or any sense

149

Delighted them in any other form;
Or that I do not yet, and ever did,
And ever will – though he do shake me off
To beggarly divorcement – love him dearly,
Comfort forswear me! Unkindness may do much,
And his unkindness may defeat my life,
160   But never taint my love. I cannot say 'whore':
It does abhor me now I speak the word;
To do the act that might the addition earn
Not the world's mass of vanity could make me.

IAGO
I pray you, be content: 'tis but his humour;
The business of the state does him offence,
And he does chide with you.

DESDEMONA
If 'twere no other –

IAGO   It is so, I warrant.
Hark how these instruments summon to supper!
The messengers of Venice stay the meat.
170   Go in, and weep not; all things shall be well.
                              Exeunt Desdemona and Emilia

        Enter Roderigo
How now, Roderigo?

RODERIGO I do not find that thou deal'st justly with
        me.
IAGO What in the contrary?
RODERIGO Every day thou daff'st me with some device,
        Iago, and rather, as it seems to me now, keep'st from me
        all conveniency, than suppliest me with the least ad-
        vantage of hope. I will indeed no longer endure it. Nor
        am I yet persuaded to put up in peace what already I
180   have foolishly suffered.
IAGO Will you hear me, Roderigo?
RODERIGO Faith, I have heard too much; for your words

and performances are no kin together.

IAGO You charge me most unjustly.

RODERIGO With naught but truth. I have wasted myself
out of my means. The jewels you have had from me to
deliver to Desdemona would half have corrupted a *nun*
votarist. You have told me she hath received them, and
returned me expectations and comforts of sudden respect
and acquaintance, but I find none.   190

IAGO Well, go to; very well.   *wondering how to deal with
this*

RODERIGO Very well, go to! I cannot go to, man, nor 'tis
not very well. Nay, I think it is scurvy and begin to
find myself fopped in it.

IAGO Very well.

RODERIGO I tell you, 'tis not very well. I will make myself
known to Desdemona. If she will return me my jewels,   *Iago's*
I will give over my suit and repent my unlawful solicita-
tion. If not, assure yourself I will seek satisfaction of *Crisis!*
you.   200

IAGO You have said now.

RODERIGO Ay, and said nothing but what I protest
intendment of doing.

IAGO Why, now I see there's mettle in thee; and even from *quick
this instant do build on thee a better opinion than ever thinking*
before. Give me thy hand, Roderigo. Thou hast taken
against me a most just exception; but yet I protest I have
dealt most directly in thy affair.

RODERIGO It hath not appeared.

IAGO I grant indeed it hath not appeared; and your sus-   210
picion is not without wit and judgement. But, Roderigo,
if thou hast that in thee indeed, which I have greater
reason to believe now than ever – I mean purpose,
courage, and valour – this night show it. If thou the
next night following enjoy not Desdemona, take me from *d/irony
this world with treachery, and devise engines for my life. – will happen*

? Cynicism of Iago's promises

RODERIGO Well, what is it? Is it within reason and compass?

IAGO Sir, there is especial commission come from Venice
220   to depute Cassio in Othello's place.

RODERIGO Is that true? Why, then Othello and Desdemona return again to Venice.

Inventio

IAGO O, no: he goes into Mauritania and takes away with
him the fair Desdemona, unless his abode be lingered
here by some accident: wherein none can be so determinate as the removing of Cassio.

RODERIGO How do you mean 'removing' of him?

IAGO Why, by making him uncapable of Othello's place -
knocking out his brains.

230 RODERIGO And that you would have me to do?

IAGO Ay, if you dare do yourself a profit and a right. He
sups tonight with a harlotry; and thither will I go to
him. He knows not yet of his honourable fortune. If
you will watch his going thence - which I will fashion to
fall out between twelve and one - you may take him at
your pleasure. I will be near to second your attempt,
and he shall fall between us. Come, stand not amazed
at it, but go along with me. I will show you such a
necessity in his death that you shall think yourself
240   bound to put it on him. It is now high supper-time and
the night grows to waste. About it!

RODERIGO I will hear further reason for this.

IAGO And you shall be satisfied.   *Exeunt*

Complete this round in the scene
★ change tape

IV.3   *Enter Othello, Lodovico, Desdemona, Emilia, and attendants*

LODOVICO
I do beseech you, sir, trouble yourself no further.

OTHELLO
O, pardon me: 'twill do me good to walk.

LODOVICO

 Madam, good night. I humbly thank your ladyship.

DESDEMONA

 Your honour is most welcome.

OTHELLO   Will you walk, sir? *(with O &*
                                                        me)

 O, Desdemona!

DESDEMONA

 My lord?

OTHELLO Get you to bed on th'instant. I will be returned
    forthwith. Dismiss your attendant there. Look't be done.

DESDEMONA I will, my lord.

                    Exeunt Othello, Lodovico, and attendants

EMILIA

 How goes it now? He looks gentler than he did.   10

DESDEMONA

 He says he will return incontinent. *forthwith / double meaning*
 He hath commanded me to go to bed,
 And bade me to dismiss you.

EMILIA   Dismiss me?

DESDEMONA

 It was his bidding: therefore, good Emilia,
 Give me my nightly wearing, and adieu.
 We must not now displease him.

EMILIA

 I would you had never seen him.

DESDEMONA

 So would not I: my love doth so approve him
 That even his stubbornness, his checks, his frowns –
 Prithee, unpin me – have grace and favour in them.   20

EMILIA

 I have laid those sheets, you bade me, on the bed.

DESDEMONA

 All's one. Good faith, how foolish are our minds!
 If I do die before thee, prithee shroud me

153

In one of those same sheets.

EMILIA   Come, come, you talk.

DESDEMONA

My mother had a maid called Barbary:
She was in love: and he she loved proved mad
And did forsake her. She had a song of willow;
An old thing 'twas; but it expressed her fortune,
And she died singing it. That song tonight
Will not go from my mind: I have much to do
But to go hang my head all at one side,
And sing it like poor Barbary – prithee, dispatch.

EMILIA

Shall I go fetch your night-gown?

DESDEMONA   No, unpin me here.

This Lodovico is a proper man.

EMILIA

A very handsome man.

DESDEMONA   He speaks well.

EMILIA I know a lady in Venice would have walked bare-
foot to Palestine for a touch of his nether lip.

DESDEMONA (sings)

The poor soul sat sighing by a sycamore tree,
    Sing all a green willow;
Her hand on her bosom, her head on her knee,
    Sing willow, willow, willow;
The fresh streams ran by her and murmured her
                    moans;
    Sing willow, willow, willow;
Her salt tears fell from her and softened the stones –
    (She speaks)
Lay by these.
    (She sings)
Sing willow, willow, willow –

[margin notes: Parallel link 1310s Cassio to earlier talk of D. She chaste "he speaks well" Emilia coarsened view.]

(*She speaks*)

Prithee hie thee; he'll come anon.
    (*She sings*)
    Sing all a green willow must be my garland.
    Let nobody blame him; his scorn I approve –
    (*She speaks*)
Nay, that's not next. Hark, who is't that knocks?   50

EMILIA It's the wind.   *jumpe*

DESDEMONA (*sings*)
    I called my love false love, but what said he then?
       Sing willow, willow, willow:
    If I court moe women, you'll couch with moe men.
    (*She speaks*)
So get thee gone; good night. Mine eyes do itch:
Does that bode weeping?

EMILIA   'Tis neither here nor there.

DESDEMONA
    I have heard it said so. O, these men, these men!
    Dost thou in conscience think – tell me, Emilia –
    That there be women do abuse their husbands
    In such gross kind?   *as in the song*

EMILIA   There be some such, no question.   60

DESDEMONA
    Wouldst thou do such a deed for all the world?

EMILIA
    Why, would not you?

DESDEMONA   No, by this heavenly light.

EMILIA Nor I neither by this heavenly light: I might do't
    as well i'th'dark.

DESDEMONA Wouldst thou do such a deed for all the
    world?

EMILIA The world's a huge thing: it is a great price for a
    small vice.

DESDEMONA In troth, I think thou wouldst not.

70 EMILIA In troth I think I should, and undo't when I had
done it. Marry, I would not do such a thing for a joint
ring, nor for measures of lawn, nor for gowns, petticoats,
nor caps, nor any petty exhibition. But for all the whole
world! Ud's pity, who would not make her husband a
cuckold, to make him a monarch? I should venture
purgatory for't.

DESDEMONA Beshrew me, if I would do such a wrong for
the whole world!

EMILIA Why, the wrong is but a wrong i'th'world; and
80 having the world for your labour, 'tis a wrong in your
own world, and you might quickly make it right.

DESDEMONA I do not think there is any such woman.

EMILIA Yes, a dozen: and as many to th'vantage as would
store the world they played for.
But I do think it is their husbands' faults
If wives do fall. Say that they slack their duties,
And pour our treasures into foreign laps;
Or else break out in peevish jealousies,
Throwing restraint upon us; or say they strike us,
Or scant our former having in despite –
Why, we have galls, and though we have some grace,
Yet have we some revenge. Let husbands know
Their wives have sense like them: they see and smell,
And have their palates both for sweet and sour
As husbands have. What is it that they do,
When they change us for others? Is it sport?
I think it is. And doth affection breed it?
I think it doth. Is't frailty that thus errs?
It is so too. And have not we affections,
100 Desires for sport, and frailty, as men have?
Then let them use us well: else let them know
The ills we do, their ills instruct us so.

DESDEMONA

Good night, good night. God me such uses send,
Not to pick bad from bad, but by bad mend!   *Exeunt*

Nor to be corrupted by evil but to overcome it by good.

Enter Iago and Roderigo   V.1

IAGO

Here, stand behind this bulk: straight will he come.
Wear thy good rapier bare, and put it home.
Quick, quick; fear nothing: I'll be at thy elbow.
It makes us, or it mars us; think on that,
And fix most firm thy resolution.

RODERIGO

Be near at hand; I may miscarry in't.

IAGO

Here, at thy hand: be bold, and take thy stand.

He retires

RODERIGO

I have no great devotion to the deed,
And yet he hath given me satisfying reasons.
'Tis but a man gone. Forth my sword! He dies!   10

IAGO

I have rubbed this young quat almost to the sense,   *pimple*
And he grows angry. Now, whether he kill Cassio,   *pinch*
Or Cassio him, or each do kill the other,
Every way makes my gain. Live Roderigo,
He calls me to a restitution large
Of gold and jewels, that I bobbed from him
As gifts to Desdemona.
It must not be. If Cassio do remain
He hath a daily beauty in his life
That makes me ugly: and besides, the Moor   20

157

V.1

May unfold me to him – there stand I in much peril.
No, he must die. But soft, I hear him coming.
　　　Enter Cassio

RODERIGO

I know his gait; 'tis he. Villain, thou diest!

CASSIO

That thrust had been mine enemy indeed,
But that my coat is better than thou think'st.
I will make proof of thine.
　　　He wounds Roderigo

RODERIGO　　　　　　　O, I am slain!
　　　Iago wounds Cassio in the leg, and exit

CASSIO

I am maimed for ever. Help, ho! Murder, murder!
　　　Enter Othello, above

OTHELLO

The voice of Cassio: Iago keeps his word.

RODERIGO

O, villain that I am!

OTHELLO　　　　　　　It is even so.

CASSIO

O, help, ho! Light! A surgeon!

OTHELLO

'Tis he! O brave Iago, honest and just,
That hast such noble sense of thy friend's wrong,
Thou teachest me! Minion, your dear lies dead,
And your unblest fate hies. Strumpet, I come!
Forth of my heart those charms, thine eyes, are blotted;
Thy bed, lust-stained, shall with lust's blood be spotted.

　　　　　　　　　　　　　　Exit Othello

　　　Enter Lodovico and Gratiano

CASSIO

What, ho! No watch? No passage? Murder, murder!

GRATIANO

'Tis some mischance: the cry is very direful.

158

CASSIO

O, help!

LODOVICO

Hark!   40

RODERIGO

O wretched villain!

LODOVICO

Two or three groan. It is a heavy night.
These may be counterfeits. Let's think't unsafe
To come in to the cry without more help.

RODERIGO

Nobody come? Then shall I bleed to death.

LODOVICO

Hark!

Enter Iago, with a light

GRATIANO

Here's one comes in his shirt, with light and weapons.

IAGO

Who's there? Whose noise is this that cries on murder?

LODOVICO

We do not know.

IAGO   Did you not hear a cry?

CASSIO

Here, here: for heaven's sake help me!

IAGO   What's the matter? 50

GRATIANO

This is Othello's Ancient, as I take it.

LODOVICO

The same indeed, a very valiant fellow.   *! even lodovico*

IAGO

What are you here, that cry so grievously?

CASSIO

Iago? O, I am spoiled, undone by villains!
Give me some help.

159

IAGO

O me, Lieutenant! What villains have done this?

CASSIO

I think that one of them is hereabout
And cannot make away.

IAGO   O treacherous villains!
What are you there? Come in, and give some help.

RODERIGO

60 O, help me here!

CASSIO

That's one of them.

IAGO   O murd'rous slave! O villain!

He stabs Roderigo

RODERIGO

O damned Iago! O inhuman dog!

He faints

IAGO

Kill men i'th'dark? Where be these bloody thieves?
How silent is this town! Ho, murder, murder!

Lodovico and Gratiano come forward

What may you be? Are you of good or evil?

LODOVICO

As you shall prove us, praise us.

IAGO

Signor Lodovico?

LODOVICO

He, sir.

IAGO

I cry you mercy. Here's Cassio hurt by villains.

GRATIANO

70 Cassio?

IAGO

How is't, brother?

CASSIO
  My leg is cut in two.

IAGO   Marry, heaven forbid!
  Light, gentlemen. I'll bind it with my shirt.
      Enter Bianca

BIANCA
  What is the matter, ho? Who is't that cried?

IAGO
  Who is't that cried?

BIANCA
  O, my dear Cassio, my sweet Cassio,
  O Cassio, Cassio, Cassio!

IAGO
  O notable strumpet! Cassio, may you suspect
  Who they should be that have thus mangled you?

CASSIO
  No.   80

GRATIANO
  I am sorry to find you thus: I have been to seek you.

IAGO
  Lend me a garter: so. O, for a chair
  To bear him easily hence!

BIANCA   Alas, he faints!
  O Cassio, Cassio, Cassio!

IAGO
  Gentlemen all, I do suspect this trash   *Bianca*
  To be a party in this injury.
  Patience awhile, good Cassio. Come, come,
  Lend me a light. Know we this face or no?
  Alas, my friend, and my dear countryman
  Roderigo? No – yes, sure – O heaven, Roderigo!   90

GRATIANO
  What! Of Venice?

161

V.1

IAGO

Even he, sir. Did you know him?

GRATIANO   Know him? Ay.

IAGO

Signor Gratiano? I cry you gentle pardon.
These bloody accidents must excuse my manners
That so neglected you.

GRATIANO   I am glad to see you.

IAGO

How do you, Cassio? O, a chair, a chair!

GRATIANO

Roderigo!

[handwritten annotation: can't believe he would attack Cassio.]

IAGO

He, he, 'tis he.

Enter attendants with chair

O, that's well said, the chair!
Some good man bear him carefully from hence.
I'll fetch the General's surgeon. For you, mistress,
Save you your labour. He that lies slain here, Cassio,
Was my dear friend. What malice was between you?

CASSIO

None in the world, nor do I know the man.

IAGO

(*to Bianca*) What, look you pale? O, bear him out
        o'th'air.

Cassio is borne in. Roderigo's body is removed

Stay you, good gentlemen. Look you pale, mistress?
Do you perceive the gastness of her eye?
Nay, if you stare, we shall hear more anon.
Behold her well; I pray you look upon her.
Do you see, gentlemen? Nay, guiltiness will speak
Though tongues were out of use.

Enter Emilia

162

EMILIA

   'Las, what's the matter? What's the matter, husband?

IAGO

   Cassio hath here been set on in the dark

   By Roderigo and fellows that are scaped:

   He's almost slain and Roderigo quite.

EMILIA

   Alas, good gentleman! Alas, good Cassio!

IAGO

   This is the fruit of whoring. Prithee, Emilia, *the prostitute*

   Go know of Cassio where he supped tonight. *Bianca wanted*

   What, do you shake at that? *Cassio killed.*

BIANCA

   He supped at my house, but I therefore shake not.

IAGO

   O, did he so? I charge you go with me.   120

EMILIA

   O, fie upon thee, strumpet!

BIANCA

   I am no strumpet, but of life as honest

   As you that thus abuse me.

EMILIA   As I? Foh! Fie upon thee!

IAGO

   Kind gentlemen, let's see poor Cassio dressed.

   Come, mistress, you must tell's another tale. *Bianca.*

   Emilia, run you to the citadel,

   And tell my lord and lady what hath happed.

   Will you go on afore? (*Aside*) This is the night

   That either makes me, or fordoes me quite.   *Exeunt*

Enter Othello, with a light, Desdemona in her bed

OTHELLO

It is the cause, it is the cause, my soul:
Let me not name it to you, you chaste stars!
It is the cause. Yet I'll not shed her blood,
Nor scar that whiter skin of hers than snow,
And smooth as monumental alabaster:
Yet she must die, else she'll betray more men.
Put out the light, and then put out the light:
If I quench thee, thou flaming minister, *the torch*
I can again thy former light restore,

10   Should I repent me; but once put out thy light,
Thou cunning'st pattern of excelling nature,
I know not where is that Promethean heat
That can thy light relume. When I have plucked thy
     rose,
I cannot give it vital growth again,
It needs must wither. I'll smell it on the tree.

     He kisses her

O balmy breath, that dost almost persuade
Justice to break her sword! One more, one more.
Be thus when thou art dead and I will kill thee,
And love thee after. One more, and this the last.

20   So sweet was ne'er so fatal. I must weep.
But they are cruel tears: this sorrow's heavenly –
It strikes where it doth love. She wakes.

DESDEMONA

Who's there? Othello?

OTHELLO

Ay, Desdemona.

DESDEMONA   Will you come to bed, my lord?

OTHELLO

Have you prayed tonight, Desdemon?

DESDEMONA   Ay, my lord.

OTHELLO

  If you bethink yourself of any crime
  Unreconciled as yet to heaven and grace,
  Solicit for it straight.

DESDEMONA

  Alack, my lord, what may you mean by that?

OTHELLO

  Well, do it, and be brief; I will walk by: 30
  I would not kill thy unprepared spirit;
  No – heaven forfend! – I would not kill thy soul.

DESDEMONA

  Talk you of killing?

OTHELLO   Ay, I do.

DESDEMONA   Then heaven

  Have mercy on me!

OTHELLO   Amen, with all my heart!

DESDEMONA

  If you say so, I hope you will not kill me.

OTHELLO

  Hum!

DESDEMONA

  And yet I fear you: for you're fatal then
  When your eyes roll so. Why I should fear I know not,
  Since guiltiness I know not; but yet I feel I fear.

OTHELLO

  Think on thy sins.

DESDEMONA   They are loves I bear to you.   40

OTHELLO

  Ay, and for that thou diest.

DESDEMONA

  That death's unnatural that kills for loving.
  Alas, why gnaw you so your nether lip?
  Some bloody passion shakes your very frame:
  These are portènts; but yet I hope, I hope

They do not point on me.

OTHELLO   Peace, and be still!

DESDEMONA

I will – so. What's the matter?

OTHELLO

That handkerchief which I so loved and gave thee,
Thou gav'st to Cassio.

DESDEMONA   No, by my life and soul!

50   Send for the man and ask him.

OTHELLO   Sweet soul, take heed,
Take heed of perjury: thou art on thy death-bed.

DESDEMONA

Ay, but not yet to die.

OTHELLO   Yes, presently.
Therefore confess thee freely of thy sin;
For to deny each article with oath
Cannot remove nor choke the strong conception
That I do groan withal. Thou art to die.

DESDEMONA

Then Lord have mercy on me!

OTHELLO   I say, amen.

DESDEMONA

And have you mercy too! I never did
Offend you in my life; never loved Cassio
60   But with such general warranty of heaven
As I might love. I never gave him token.

OTHELLO

By heaven, I saw my handkerchief in's hand!
O perjured woman! Thou dost stone my heart,
And mak'st me call what I intend to do
A murder, which I thought a sacrifice.
I saw the handkerchief.

DESDEMONA   He found it then.
I never gave it him. Send for him hither.

166

Let him confess a truth.

OTHELLO   He hath confessed.

DESDEMONA

What, my lord?

OTHELLO

That he hath used thee.

DESDEMONA   How? Unlawfully?   70

OTHELLO

Ay.

DESDEMONA

He will not say so.

OTHELLO   No, his mouth is stopped:

Honest Iago hath ta'en order for't.

DESDEMONA

O, my fear interprets! What, is he dead?

*Not so. O is
mistaken.*

OTHELLO

Had all his hairs been lives, my great revenge

Had stomach for them all.

DESDEMONA

Alas, he is betrayed, and I undone. ———

OTHELLO

Out, strumpet! Weep'st thou for him to my face?

DESDEMONA

O banish me, my lord, but kill me not!

OTHELLO

Down, strumpet!   80

DESDEMONA

Kill me tomorrow: let me live tonight!

OTHELLO

Nay, if you strive –

DESDEMONA

But half an hour!

OTHELLO   Being done, there is no pause.

DESDEMONA

But while I say one prayer!

OTHELLO   It is too late.

DESDEMONA

O Lord, Lord, Lord!

He smothers her

EMILIA

(*without*) My lord, my lord! What, ho! My lord, my
lord!

OTHELLO

What noise is this? Not dead? Not yet quite dead?
I, that am cruel, am yet merciful:
I would not have thee linger in thy pain.

90   So, so.

EMILIA (*without*) What, ho! My lord, my lord!

OTHELLO   Who's there?

EMILIA

(*without*) O, good my lord, I'd speak a word with you.

OTHELLO

Yes, 'tis Emilia. – By and by. – She's dead.
'Tis like she comes to speak of Cassio's death:
The noise was high. Ha! No more moving?
Still as the grave. Shall she come in? Were't good?
I think she stirs again. No. What's best to do?
If she come in, she'll sure speak to my wife –
My wife! My wife! What wife? I have no wife.
O, insupportable! O heavy hour!

100   Methinks it should be now a huge eclipse
Of sun and moon, and that th'affrighted globe
Should yawn at alteration.

EMILIA   I do beseech you

That I may speak with you. O, good my lord!

OTHELLO

I had forgot thee. O, come in, Emilia.

Soft; by and by. Let me the curtains draw.
Where art thou? (*He unlocks door*.) What's the matter
   with thee now?
   Enter Emilia

EMILIA
   O, my good lord, yonder's foul murder done.

OTHELLO
   What! Now?

EMILIA
   But now, my lord.

OTHELLO
   It is the very error of the moon;   110
   She comes more nearer earth than she was wont,
   And makes men mad.

EMILIA
   Cassio, my lord, hath killed a young Venetian
   Called Roderigo.

OTHELLO   Roderigo killed?
   And Cassio killed?   *as he had hoped from Iago*

EMILIA   No, Cassio is not killed.

OTHELLO
   Not Cassio killed! Then murder's out of tune,
   And sweet revenge grows harsh.   *Disappointed.*

DESDEMONA
   O, falsely, falsely murdered!

EMILIA   O Lord! What cry is that?

OTHELLO
   That? What?

EMILIA
   Out and alas, that was my lady's voice!   120
      She draws back the curtains
   Help, help, ho, help! O, lady, speak again!
   Sweet Desdemona, O sweet mistress, speak!

DESDEMONA

A guiltless death I die.

EMILIA

O, who hath done this deed?

DESDEMONA

Nobody – I myself – farewell.

Commend me to my kind lord – O, farewell! *She dies*

OTHELLO

Why, how should she be murdered?

EMILIA   Alas, who knows?

OTHELLO

You heard her say herself it was not I.

EMILIA

She said so: I must needs report the truth.

OTHELLO

130 She's like a liar gone to burning hell:

'Twas I that killed her.

EMILIA   O, the more angel she,

And you the blacker devil!

OTHELLO

She turned to folly; and she was a whore.

EMILIA

Thou dost belie her, and thou art a devil.

OTHELLO

She was false as water.

EMILIA   Thou art rash as fire to say

That she was false. O, she was heavenly true!

OTHELLO

Cassio did top her: ask thy husband else.

O, I were damned beneath all depth in hell

But that I did proceed upon just grounds

140 To this extremity. Thy husband knew it all.

EMILIA

My husband!

OTHELLO   Thy husband.

EMILIA   That she was false to wedlock?

OTHELLO

Ay, with Cassio. Nay, had she been true,
If heaven would make me such another world
Of one entire and perfect chrysolite,
I'd not have sold her for it.

EMILIA   My husband!

OTHELLO

Ay, 'twas he that told me on her first.
An honest man he is, and hates the slime
That sticks on filthy deeds.

EMILIA   My husband!

OTHELLO

What needs this iterance, woman? I say thy husband.

EMILIA

O mistress, villainy hath made mocks with love!   150
My husband say that she was false?

OTHELLO   He, woman;
I say thy husband; dost understand the word?
My friend, thy husband, honest, honest Iago.

EMILIA

If he say so, may his pernicious soul
Rot half a grain a day! He lies to th'heart.
She was too fond of her most filthy bargain.

OTHELLO

Ha!

EMILIA

Do thy worst:
This deed of thine is no more worthy heaven
Than thou wast worthy her.

OTHELLO   Peace, you were best.   160

EMILIA

Thou hast not half that power to do me harm
As I have to be hurt. O gull! O dolt!
As ignorant as dirt! Thou hast done a deed –

Comale

I care not for thy sword – I'll make thee known,
Though I lost twenty lives. Help! Help, ho! Help!
Reversion to racial sash The Moor hath killed my mistress! Murder! Murder!

Enter Montano, Gratiano, and Iago

MONTANO

What is the matter? How now, General?

EMILIA

O, are you come, Iago? You have done well,
That men must lay their murders on your neck.

GRATIANO

170   What is the matter?

EMILIA

Disprove this villain, if thou be'st a man:
He says thou told'st him that his wife was false.
I know thou didst not: thou'rt not such a villain.
Speak, for my heart is full.

IAGO

I told him what I thought, and told no more
Than what he found himself was apt and true.

EMILIA

But did you ever tell him she was false?

IAGO

I did.

EMILIA

You told a lie, an odious damnèd lie:
180   Upon my soul, a lie, a wicked lie!
She false with Cassio! Did you say with Cassio?

IAGO

With Cassio, mistress! Go to, charm your tongue.

EMILIA

I will not charm my tongue; I am bound to speak:
My mistress here lies murdered in her bed.

ALL
O heavens forfend!

EMILIA
And your reports have set the murder on.

OTHELLO
Nay, stare not masters: it is true indeed.

GRATIANO
'Tis a strange truth.

MONTANO
O monstrous act!

EMILIA   Villainy, villainy, villainy!
I think upon't, I think – I smell't – O villainy!   190
I thought so then; I'll kill myself for grief.
O villainy, villainy!

[handwritten: when O. was suspicious]

IAGO
What, are you mad? I charge you get you home.

EMILIA
Good gentlemen, let me have leave to speak.
'Tis proper I obey him, but not now.
Perchance, Iago, I will ne'er go home.

OTHELLO
(*falling on bed*) O! O! O!

EMILIA   Nay, lay thee down and roar,
For thou hast killed the sweetest innocent
That e'er did lift up eye.

OTHELLO (*rising*)   O, she was foul!
I scarce did know you, uncle; there lies your niece,   200
Whose breath indeed these hands have newly stopped.
I know this act shows horrible and grim.

[handwritten: Gratiano, D's uncle.]

GRATIANO
Poor Desdemon, I am glad thy father's dead:
Thy match was mortal to him, and pure grief
Shore his old thread in twain. Did he live now,
This sight would make him do a desperate turn,

[handwritten: Brab he meant had killed Brabantio with grief]

[handwritten: Brab's death due to grief over her marriage to O.]

173

V.2

Yea, curse his better angel from his side,
And fall to reprobance.

OTHELLO

'Tis pitiful: but yet Iago knows

210   That she with Cassio hath the act of shame
A thousand times committed. Cassio confessed it,
And she did gratify his amorous works
With that recognizance and pledge of love
Which I first gave her. I saw it in his hand:
It was a handkerchief, an antique token
My father gave my mother.

EMILIA   O God! O heavenly Powers!

IAGO

Zounds, hold your peace!

EMILIA   'Twill out, 'twill out. I peace?
No, I will speak as liberal as the north;
Let heaven, and men, and devils, let them all,

220   All, all cry shame against me, yet I'll speak.

IAGO

Be wise, and get you home.

EMILIA   I will not.

Iago draws his sword

GRATIANO   Fie!
Your sword upon a woman!

EMILIA

O thou dull Moor, that handkerchief thou speak'st of
I found by fortune and did give my husband,
For often, with a solemn earnestness –
More than indeed belonged to such a trifle –
He begged of me to steal it.

IAGO   Villainous whore!

EMILIA

She give it Cassio? No, alas, I found it
And I did give't my husband.

174

IAGO   Filth, thou liest!

EMILIA

By heaven I do not, I do not, gentlemen.
O murderous coxcomb, what should such a fool   *gullible fool*
Do with so good a wife?   *Othello*

OTHELLO   Are there no stones in heaven   *should*
But what serve for the thunder? Precious villain!   *fall on Iago*

He runs at Iago; Montano disarms him;
Iago stabs Emilia from behind and exit

GRATIANO

The woman falls: sure he hath killed his wife.

EMILIA

Ay, ay: O, lay me by my mistress' side.

GRATIANO

He's gone, but his wife's killed.

MONTANO

'Tis a notorious villain. Take you this weapon,   *O's sword*
Which I have here recovered from the Moor.
Come guard the door without: let him not pass,   *O.*
But kill him rather. I'll after that same villain,   230
For 'tis a damnèd slave.

Exeunt Montano and Gratiano

OTHELLO   I am not valiant neither,
But every puny whipster gets my sword.
But why should honour outlive honesty?   *the traitor.*
Let it go all.

EMILIA   What did thy song bode, lady?
Hark, canst thou hear me? I will play the swan
And die in music. (*Singing*) Willow, willow, willow.
Moor, she was chaste; she loved thee, cruel Moor,
So come my soul to bliss, as I speak true;
So speaking as I think, I die, I die.   *She dies*

OTHELLO

I have another weapon in this chamber: 250

It was a sword of Spain, the ice-brook's temper.
O, here it is. Uncle, I must come forth.

GRATIANO

Let me out.

(*within*) If thou attempt it, it will cost thee dear;
Thou hast no weapon, and perforce must suffer.

OTHELLO

Look in upon me then, and speak with me,
Or naked as I am I will assault thee.

    Enter Gratiano

GRATIANO

What is the matter?

OTHELLO   Behold, I have a weapon:
A better never did itself sustain
Upon a soldier's thigh. I have seen the day
260   That with this little arm and this good sword,
I have made my way through more impediments
Than twenty times your stop. But, O vain boast! –
end of his pride in his valour   Who can control his fate? – 'Tis not so now.
Be not afraid, though you do see me weaponed:
Here is my journey's end, here is my butt
And very sea-mark of my utmost sail.
Do you go back dismayed? 'Tis a lost fear:
Man but a rush against Othello's breast,
And he retires. Where should Othello go?

    He goes to the bed

270   Now, how dost thou look now? O ill-starred wench!
Pale as thy smock! When we shall meet at compt
This look of thine will hurl my soul from heaven
And fiends will snatch at it. Cold, cold, my girl,
Even like thy chastity.
O cursèd, cursèd slave! Whip me, ye devils,
From the possession of this heavenly sight!
Blow me about in winds! Roast me in sulphur!
Wash me in steep-down gulfs of liquid fire!

O Desdemon! Dead Desdemon! Dead! O! O!

Enter Lodovico, Cassio in a chair, Montano and Iago
with officers

LODOVICO

Where is this rash and most unfortunate man?   280

OTHELLO

That's he that was Othello: here I am.

LODOVICO

Where is that viper? Bring the villain forth.

OTHELLO   *— to see if they are cloven*

I look down towards his feet; but that's a fable.
If that thou be'st a devil, I cannot kill thee.

He wounds Iago

LODOVICO

Wrench his sword from him.

IAGO   I bleed, sir, but not killed.

OTHELLO

I am not sorry neither; I'd have thee live,
For in my sense 'tis happiness to die.

LODOVICO

O, thou Othello, that wast once so good,   *as the dupe of*
Fallen in the practice of a damnèd slave,   *Iago.*
What shall be said to thee?

OTHELLO   Why, anything: 290
An honourable murderer, if you will:
For naught did I in hate, but all in honour.

LODOVICO

This wretch hath part confessed his villainy.
Did you and he consent in Cassio's death?

OTHELLO

Ay.

CASSIO

Dear General, I never gave you cause.

OTHELLO

I do believe it, and I ask your pardon.
Will you, I pray, demand that demi-devil
Why he hath thus ensnared my soul and body?

IAGO

300   Demand me nothing; what you know, you know:
From this time forth I never will speak word.

LODOVICO

What! Not to pray?

GRATIANO

Torments will ope your lips.

OTHELLO   Well, thou dost best.

LODOVICO

Sir, you shall understand what hath befallen,
Which, as I think, you know not. Here is a letter
Found in the pocket of the slain Roderigo,
And here another: the one of them imports
The death of Cassio, to be undertook
By Roderigo.

OTHELLO   O villain!

CASSIO   Most heathenish and most gross!

LODOVICO

310   Now here's another discontented paper
Found in his pocket too; and this, it seems
Roderigo meant to have sent this damnèd villain,
But that, belike, Iago, in the nick,
Came in and satisfied him.

OTHELLO   O the pernicious caitiff!

How came you, Cassio, by that handkerchief
That was my wife's?

CASSIO   I found it in my chamber;
And he himself confessed but even now
That there he dropped it for a special purpose
Which wrought to his desire.

OTHELLO   O fool, fool, fool!

CASSIO

  There is besides, in Roderigo's letter,   *Written*   320
  How he upbraids Iago, that he made him   *when I was*
  Brave me upon the watch, whereon it came   *sceptical of Iago.*
  That I was cast; and even but now he spake   *before his fatal*
  After long seeming dead – Iago hurt him,   *acquiescence in*
  Iago set him on.   *stabbing Cassio*

LODOVICO

  You must forsake this room and go with us.   *to Othello.*
  Your power and your command is taken off
  And Cassio rules in Cyprus. For this slave,
  If there be any cunning cruelty
  That can torment him much, and hold him long,   330
  It shall be his. You shall close prisoner rest,   *Othello for*
  Till that the nature of your fault be known   *trial in*
  To the Venetian state. Come, bring him away.   *Venice*

OTHELLO

  Soft you; a word or two before you go.
  I have done the state some service and they know't:
  No more of that. I pray you in your letters
  When you shall these unlucky deeds relate
  Speak of me as I am: nothing extenuate,
  Nor set down aught in malice. Then must you speak
  Of one that loved not wisely, but too well;   340
  Of one, not easily jealous but, being wrought,
  Perplexed in the extreme; of one whose hand
  Like the base Indian threw a pearl away
  Richer than all his tribe; of one whose subdued eyes,
  Albeit unusèd to the melting mood,
  Drop tears as fast as the Arabian trees
  Their med'cinable gum. Set you down this:
  And say, besides, that in Aleppo once
  Where a malignant and a turbaned Turk

to give himself the power to kill himself

350   Beat a Venetian and traduced the state,
I took by th'throat the circumcisèd dog
And smote him thus.

           He stabs himself

LODOVICO
     O bloody period!

GRATIANO   All that's spoke is marred!

OTHELLO
     I kissed thee, ere I killed thee: no way but this,
Killing myself, to die upon a kiss.

           He falls on the bed and dies

Un Bacio

CASSIO
     This did I fear, but thought he had no weapon,
For he was great of heart.

LODOVICO   O, Spartan dog,
More fell than anguish, hunger, or the sea,
Look on the tragic loading of this bed:

360   This is thy work. The object poisons sight:
Let it be hid.

        The curtains are drawn

           Gratiano, keep the house
And seize upon the fortunes of the Moor, *Cassio*
For they succeed on you. To you, Lord Governor,
Remains the censure of this hellish villain:
The time, the place, the torture, O, enforce it!
Myself will straight aboard, and to the state
This heavy act with heavy heart relate.   *Exeunt*

COMMENTARY

I.1
The play opens at night, in the street outside Brabantio's house in the middle of a conversation between Iago and Roderigo, described in the Folio (F) list of characters as 'a Villaine' and 'a gull'd Gentleman'. Although the opening scenes of Shakespeare's plays are expository, the facts are here distorted by Iago's envy and by his anxiety not to be deprived of Roderigo's money. Iago has been as surprised as his dupe by Desdemona's marriage.

4
'Sblood God's blood. This and other oaths were omitted in F because of the new regulations against profanity. Iago's oaths contrast with Roderigo's feeble 'Tush'.

8-33
Despise me, if I do not . . . his Moorship's Ancient. We cannot assume that Iago's account is accurate or that the main cause of his hatred of Othello is Cassio's promotion. See Introduction, p. 16.

13
bombast circumstance bombastic beating about the bush

14
stuffed. Bombast was originally cotton used for stuffing quilts and clothes.

16
Non-suits rejects the suit of
Certes certainly

19
arithmetician. Iago means that Cassio's knowledge of war was theoretical.

21
A fellow almost damned in a fair wife. Possibly at this point in the play Shakespeare intended to give Cassio a wife and afterwards decided to fuse the harlot and the lady (*donna*) of the source. There were Italian and English proverbs on the damnation involved in having a fair wife - because she was certain to be seduced.

24
theoric theory

25
togèd. Shakespeare is thinking of the Venetian government in terms of ancient Roman senators, wearing togas.

The F reading, 'tongued', accepted by few editors, would mean that the senators could prattle about military matters without having any practical experience of them.

30   *leed* cut off from the wind. This is clearly the intention of the Quarto (Q) 'led'; the F reading 'be be-leed' is awkward to speak. Iago's matter-of-fact nautical imagery contrasts with the imaginative sea-imagery of Othello.

31   *counter-caster* one who reckons with counters

33   *Ancient* ensign

36   *letter and affection* influence and nepotism. But Iago had himself pulled strings (see line 8).

37   *gradation* process of advancing step by step

39   *affined* constrained

44   *truly* faithfully
     shall mark cannot help noticing

45   *knave* servant

47   *ass.* Both Iago and Othello make frequent use of animal imagery. See Introduction, p. 22.

48   *cashiered!* he is cashiered. The elliptical expression is characteristic of Iago.

49   *Whip me* (ethical dative)

52   *shows* appearances

53   *lined their coats* feathered their nests

58   *Were I the Moor, I would not be Iago* if I were the General, I would not wish to be a subordinate

61   *peculiar* personal

63   *figure* shape, intention

64   *compliment extern* outward show

66   *I am not what I am.* This is thought by some to be a parody of Exodus 3.14, 'I am that I am', and by others to mean 'I am not what I seem to be'. Iago means merely that, if he were to wear his heart on his sleeve, he would cease to be himself.

67   *full* perfect
     thick-lips. This is the first indication that Othello is negroid.

67   *owe* own
68   *If he can carry't thus* if he can get away with it
     her father (Desdemona's father, Brabantio)
73   *chances* possibilities
76   *timorous* causing fear
82   (stage direction) *at a window.* On the Elizabethan stage
     the window would be at the side on the balcony level.
87   *Zounds* God's wounds
     robbed ... gown. A quibble may be intended on 'robbed'
     and 'robed'.
88   *burst* broken
90   *tupping* covering
91   *snorting* snoring
92   *devil.* The devil was depicted as black.
100 *distempering* intoxicating
101 *bravery* show of courage
102 *start* startle
103 *Sir, sir, sir.* Roderigo's words are extra-metrical, and
     Brabantio continues without a pause.
107 *grange* country house
108 *simple* sincere
112 *Barbary.* The Barbary coast, North Africa, was famous
     for horse-breeding. Iago is, of course, referring to the
     Moor.
114 *jennet* a small Spanish horse
     germans near relations
117–18 *making the beast with two backs* engaging in sexual inter-
     course. In fact, as we learn later, Othello's marriage is
     consummated in Act II.
119 *You are a Senator.* Many editors assume that Iago sup-
     presses an uncomplimentary word, but he may either be
     ironically polite or pretending that 'Senator' is uncom-
     plimentary.
123 *partly* in some degree (from your apparent lack of con-
     cern)
124 *odd–even* between midnight and 1 a.m.
126 *knave* servant

127   *Moor –* . Roderigo does not complete his sentence.

128   *allowance* permission

132   *from the sense of all civility* contrary to good manners

137   *extravagant and wheeling* vagrant

143   *accident* event

149   *check* reprimand

150   *cast* dismiss
       embarked engaged

152   *stand in act* are in progress

153   *fathom* ability. This is one of Iago's admissions about the man he hates.

159   *Sagittary* (the name of the inn or the house where Othello and Desdemona are lodging)

160   (stage direction) *night-gown* dressing-gown

162   *despisèd time*. A father whose daughter married without his permission would be regarded as dishonoured.

172   *charms* enchantments (the first of many references to witchcraft)

173   *property* nature

183   *officers of night*. These are mentioned in *The Commonwealth and Government of Venice*. See Introduction, p. 12.

I.2   The calm dignity of Othello on his first appearance contrasts with what Iago and Brabantio have said about him in the previous scene.

1-10   *Though in the trade of war . . . I did full hard forbear him.* Iago is posing as a loyal follower of Othello, in accordance with the hypocritical course of conduct outlined in the first scene, and ascribing to Roderigo his own descriptions of the Moor. He has apparently told Othello that Roderigo was responsible for informing Brabantio of Desdemona's elopement.

2   *very stuff* essence (but carrying on the metaphor of 'trade')

3   *contrived* (accent on first syllable)

5   *yerked* thrust

10   *full hard* with great difficulty

12   *Magnifico* (Brabantio's title)

13-14   *voice potential* | *As double as the Duke's.* Shakespeare
        would have found several passages in Lewkenor's
        translation of Contarini's *Commonwealth and Govern-
        ment of Venice* about the powers of the Duke, and
        though 'voice' often means 'vote' in Shakespeare's
        plays, the Duke did not have two votes. Either Shake-
        speare was careless in his perusal of the book, or he
        meant simply that Brabantio's voice was as influential
        as the Duke's and twice as influential as those of the
        other Senators.

13   *potential* powerful

18   *signory* Venetian government

19   *yet to know* not yet known

21   *provulgate* publish abroad. As this is a rarer word than
        'promulgate' (F), it is unlikely to have been a misprint.

22   *siege* rank
        demerits deserts

23   *unbonneted* without my hat on, with all due modesty

26   *unhousèd* without a house

27   *circumscription and confine* restriction and restraint

28   *yond* yonder

31   *parts* natural gifts
        perfect soul clear conscience

33   *Janus* (a two-faced Roman god – the oath is appropriate
        to the two-faced Iago)

39   *divine* guess

40   *heat* urgency

44   *hotly* urgently

50   *carack* large ship

52   *who* whom

53   *Marry* the Virgin Mary (with a quibble on the word)
        Have with you I'll go with you

58   *Come, sir, I am for you.* Iago pretends to fight Roderigo.

59   *Keep up your bright swords, for the dew will rust them.* This

185

exhibits Othello's calm authority rather than his supposed tendency to self-dramatization.

63   *enchanted.* See note to I.1.172.

67   *opposite* opposed

70   *guardage* guardianship

72   *gross in sense* quite obvious

74   *minerals.* This is one of many references to poison.

75   *motion* impulses, faculties

77   *attach* arrest

79   *arts inhibited* the black art

        out of warrant unwarrantable

86   *direct session* immediate sitting of court

95   *idle* trifling

99   *Bondslaves and pagans shall our statesmen be.* This reference to slavery was perhaps suggested by the Venetian constitution. Brabantio implies that if blackamoors are allowed to intermarry with Venetian citizens, either the Senators would be reduced to the level of slaves or else the government would be taken over by former slaves.

I.3   The early part of this scene, concerned with the Turkish danger, is a means of building up Othello's reputation as a soldier; the second part, containing Othello's defence of his wooing, is an effective rebuttal of Iago's slanders and Brabantio's accusations of witchcraft, and it shows that Desdemona was half the wooer; the third part, after the departure of the Senators, reveals Iago's plot to retain his hold over Roderigo and the birth of his scheme to make Othello jealous of Cassio. This is prepared for by the accounts of Cassio in the first scene and his brief and colourless appearance in the second.

1   *composition* consistency

2   *disproportioned* inconsistent

5   *jump* tally

6–7   *where the aim reports | 'Tis oft with difference* where there are discrepancies between one report and another

10   *I do not so secure me in the error* I do not feel myself so secure from the discrepancy between the various reports as not to believe the thing common to all

11   *approve* endorse

18   *assay* test

    pageant show

19   *in false gaze* looking in the wrong direction

20   *importancy* importance

23   *with more facile question bear it* capture it more easily

24   *brace* readiness

26   *dressed in* equipped with

30   *wage* risk

35   *injointed* united

37   *re-stem* re-trace

50   *I did not see you.* The Duke has been absorbed in his papers.

57   *engluts* swallows up

64   *Sans* without

67–9   *the bloody book of law | You shall yourself read in the bitter letter | After your own sense* you shall be judge in your own cause and sentence the guilty one to death

69   *proper* own

70   *Stood* were accused

80   *head and front* height and breadth

81   *Rude am I in my speech.* There is nothing in the splendid poetry put into Othello's mouth to support this modest admission; but he is given an exotic vocabulary and a style which distinguishes his speech from that of the other characters.

90   *round* plain

92   *conjuration* incantation

95   *motion* movement of the soul, impulse

96   *herself* itself

105   *conjured* induced by magic spells (the accent is on the second syllable)

107   *more wider* fuller

108   *thin habits* tenuous arguments
      likelihoods hypotheses

109   *modern* ordinary

113   *question* talk

122-3 *as truly as to heaven | I do confess the vices of my blood.*
      Othello, as we are reminded often, is a Christian.

128   *Still* continually

138   *portance* behaviour
      travels'. This reading is superior to that of F, since
      'Trauellers' would imply that Othello's story had been
      embroidered.

139-44 *Wherein of antres vast and deserts idle . . . Do grow beneath
      their shoulders.* These details were derived from Pliny's
      Natural History and from Elizabethan narratives of
      travel.

139   *antres* caves
      idle uninhabited, sterile

141   *hint* occasion

143   *Anthropophagi* man-eaters

150   *pliant* favourable

152   *dilate* relate in full

153   *by parcels* piecemeal

154   *intentively* attentively, continuously

158   *sighs.* The F reading, 'kisses', is obviously impossible.

162   *her.* Desdemona wished she could have been a man to
      have had such adventures; she was not suggesting that
      she would like to have such a husband.

165   *hint* opportunity. Othello is not suggesting that Des-
      demona was fishing for a proposal, although the pre-
      vious words seem to be a fairly direct hint.

171   *take up this mangled matter at the best* make the best of a
      bad job

180   *education* upbringing

181   *learn* teach

186   *challenge* claim

187   *bu'y* be with you

189   *get* beget

193   *For your sake* on your own account
195   *escape* elopement
196   *clogs* (blocks of wood fastened to legs)
198   *grise* step
200   *When remedies are past . . . piecèd through the ear.* The
-217   rhymed verse suggests that both the Duke and Braban-
       tio are indulging in proverbial wisdom, and the speeches
       have a choric effect.
207   *bootless* vain
217   *piecèd* mended
       through the ear by listening to consolation
218   *I humbly beseech you to proceed to th'affairs of state.* The
       drop into prose indicates the change of subject.
220   *fortitude* strength
222   *allowed* acknowledged
       opinion public opinion
223   *more safer* safer
224   *slubber* spoil
225   *stubborn* inflexible
227   *tyrant, custom* (proverbial)
229   *agnize* acknowledge
230-31 *A natural and prompt alacrity | I find in hardness* that I
       am eager to embrace hardship
233   *bending to your state* bowing to your office
234   *disposition* arrangements
235   *Due reference of place* treatment as becomes her rank
       exhibition financial provision
236   *besort* retinue
237   *levels* fits
242   *unfolding* proposal
       prosperous favourable
243   *charter* pledge
246   *storm.* The Q reading 'scorne' is attractive, but 'storm'
       is supported by Lewkenor, from whom the phrase is
       echoed.
247-8 *My heart's subdued | Even to the very quality of my lord*
       I am in love with Othello's virtues

253   *moth* (condemned to useless idleness)

254   *rites* (of marriage). Desdemona's frankness about sex
       contrasts with her husband's later protestations that
       he is anxious merely for companionship; but several
       editors prefer 'rights' – her right to share Othello's life.

257   *Let her have your voice.* Some critics suppose that the
       Senators here show astonishment that Othello should
       ask to take his wife on active service; but if this had been
       Shakespeare's intention he would have made the Duke
       express surprise.

260   *comply with* satisfy
       affects desires

261   *In me defunct – and proper satisfaction.* The line is prob-
       ably corrupt in both texts, but the general meaning is
       clear. Othello is explaining that he is no longer a young
       man swayed by passion, and that he wants Desdemona's
       companionship more than the gratification of his own
       'proper' desires. Those who think that Othello is de-
       ceived about himself fasten on this line.

263   *defend* forbid

266   *seel* blind (from the practice of sewing up the eyelids of
       a hawk)

267   *speculative and officed instruments* eyes and other facul-
       ties

268   *disports* sexual pleasures

269   *skillet* (small metal pot, used in cooking)

270   *indign* unworthy

271   *estimation* reputation

279   *quality and respect* importance and relevance

280   *import* concern

281   *A man he is of honesty and trust.* The audience is aware
       that Othello is completely deceived about Iago and
       has no idea that he bears resentment at being passed
       over.

286   *delighted* delightful

287   *far more fair than black.* This contrast between black
       and white recurs frequently throughout the play.

289-90 *Look to her, Moor, if thou hast eyes to see. | She has deceived her father, and may thee.* Iago remembers this couplet (see III.3.204).

294 *in the best advantage* at the best opportunity

296 *direction* instructions

298 *Iago . . . the world's light.* On Shakespeare's unlocalized
-398 stage, the scene ceases to be the council-chamber when Roderigo and Iago are left alone.

302 *incontinently* forthwith

306 *prescription.* This is a quibble on medical prescription and 'immemorial right' (A. Walker).

312 *guinea-hen* prostitute

320 *gender* kind

322 *corrigible authority* corrective power

323 *beam* balance

327 *unbitted* unbridled

328 *sect* cutting

331-2 *It is merely a lust of the blood and a permission of the will.* This is Iago's real opinion, though he is using it to corrupt Roderigo. He has been paid by Roderigo to arrange a marriage with Desdemona: he now holds out the hope that she can be seduced.

334 *perdurable* long-lasting

335 *stead* benefit

337 *defeat thy favour* disguise your face
usurped wrongly appropriated (because Roderigo is unmanly) or false

341 *sequestration* separation

344 *locusts* (cobs of the carob tree)

345 *acerbe* bitter (the reading of F)
coloquintida colocynth (bitter apple used as purgative drug)

349 *Make* raise

350 *erring* wandering, sinful

361 *hearted* heart-felt

362 *conjunctive* allied

365 *Traverse!* about turn!

370   *betimes* early

377–98   *Thus do I ever make my fool my purse ... the world's light.*
In Iago's soliloquy we see him for the first time without a mask.

384   *holds me well* esteems me

386   *proper* handsome

387   *plume up* set a feather in the cap of

391   *dispose* disposition

393–4   *The Moor is of a free and open nature, | That thinks men honest that but seem to be so.* This is another tribute from the villain about the hero, though it is said with a sneer.

397–8   *Hell and night | Must bring this monstrous birth to the world's light.* Iago deliberately chooses evil.

II.1   The rest of the play is set in Cyprus. Enough time has elapsed to enable the chief characters to sail to the island from Venice. The scene is near the harbour. The function of the storm is to show, by the anxiety for Othello's safety, the esteem in which he is held, to exhibit the mutual love of Othello and Desdemona, to dispose of the Turkish danger, which is now dramatically unnecessary, and to symbolize the tempest of passion which is soon to overwhelm Othello.

7   *ruffianed* raged

8   *mountains* mountainous seas

10   *segregation* dispersal

11   *banning* cursing. This reading is superior to the colourless 'foaming'.

13   *monstrous mane.* The seas are compared to a wild beast.

15   *guards of th'ever-fixèd Pole* (two stars in the Little Bear known as the Guardians)

16   *molestation* disturbance

17   *enchafèd* angry

22   *designment* design. The Turkish danger, necessary for displaying Othello's reputation, is ended before his arrival in Cyprus.

23   *sufferance* damage

26   *Veronesa.* Presumably this was a vessel fitted out by
      Verona, which belonged to Venice; but it has been sug-
      gested that the word should be *verrinessa*, or cutter.
      (Shakespeare, to judge from *The Two Gentlemen of
      Verona*, thought that town was a port.)

30   *'tis a worthy governor* (another tribute to Othello)

32   *sadly* gravely

39   *th'aerial blue* the sky

40   *An indistinct regard* indistinguishable

41   *expectancy* expectation

42   *more arrivance* the arrival of more ships

49   *allowance* reputation

50–51 *not surfeited to death,* | *Stand in bold cure* are not exces-
      sive, but healthy

55   *My hopes do shape him for* I hope it is

60   *is your General wived?* There has been no previous men-
      tion of Othello's marriage. Possibly some lines have
      dropped out, for Montano has had no private conversa-
      tion with Cassio.

62   *paragons* equals or excels

64–5 *And in th'essential vesture of creation* | *Does tire the
      ingener* 'in real beauty or outward form goes beyond the
      power of the artist's inventive or expressive pencil'
      (Hudson). But 'ingener' is an emendation of 'Ingeniuer'
      and 'tyre' can mean 'attire', as well as 'weary'. Possibly
      'tire' was suggested by 'vesture' through an unconscious
      quibble.

69   *guttered* with gullies, jagged

70   *enscarped to clog.* Nearly all editors accept 'ensteeped'
      from F but reject 'enclogge'. It seems probable that
      'enscerped' was a misprint for 'enscarped' (that is,
      shelved abruptly). This fits the rocks, if not the sands;
      and Shakespeare may have been responsible for both
      readings.

72   *mortal* deadly. Here again the alternative reading 'com-
      mon' makes good sense.

76   *footing* landing

77   *se'nnight* week

80   *Make love's quick pants.* This weak phrase was substituted for an even feebler phrase in Q.

87   *Enwheel* encircle

94   *greeting* (by firing a salvo)

99   *courtesy.* Kissing was a normal method of greeting, and does not imply that Cassio was flirting with Emilia.

107   *chides with thinking* does not utter her shrewish thoughts

108   *pictures* (that is, silent)

109   *bells* (that is, noisy)

111   *housewives* hussies

119   *assay* try

121-2   *I am not merry, but I do beguile | The thing I am by seeming otherwise.* This is merely an explanation to the audience, so that Desdemona should not appear too little concerned for Othello's safety.

125   *as birdlime does from frieze.* Frieze or frize is a coarse cloth, and when one tries to remove birdlime from it, one pulls out the threads at the same time. So Iago's powers of invention are 'sticky'.

130   *witty* clever
       black brunette

132   *white* (with a quibble on 'wight')

135   *folly* wantonness

136   *fond* foolish

138   *foul* ugly or sluttish

144   *put on the vouch* compel the approval

152   *change the cod's head for the salmon's tail.* This passage is obscure, probably obscene, in view of the connotations of cod's 'head' and 'tail'; but it may merely mean exchange a foolish husband for a handsome lover.

157   *small beer* trivial events

160   *profane* worldly

161   *liberal* licentious

162   *home* bluntly

162-3   *relish him more in* appreciate him more in the role of

167   *gyve* fetter, ensnare

167-8   *You say true, 'tis so indeed.* This is either a comment on the animated conversation between Cassio and Desdemona or a reply (not spoken aloud) to Cassio's last remark (lines 162-3).

171   *sir* gentleman

173   *clyster-pipes* tubes used for injection (here used obscenely)

176   *fair warrior.* Othello is referring to her courage in accompanying him to the wars, and unconsciously echoing the language of sonneteers. He may also be thinking of her wish she had been a man.

183-9   *If it were now to die . . . Amen to that, sweet Powers!* (dramatic irony)

194   *set down the pegs* slacken the strings

198   *desired* liked

200   *out of fashion* unbecomingly

205   *challenge* claim

207-8   *Do thou meet me presently at the harbour.* These lines are spoken not to Roderigo, but to one of the soldiers who are to fetch Othello's luggage.

207   *presently* at once

215   *thus* (on the lips)

223   *favour* appearance

225   *conveniences* points of fitness

229   *pregnant* cogent

231   *conscionable* conscientious

233   *humane* polite
       salt lustful

235   *slipper* slippery
       occasions opportunities

236   *stamp* coin

243   *condition* characteristics

244   *fig's end* a worthless thing

247   *paddle with* stroke

254   *incorporate* bodily

259   *tainting* sneering at

261   *minister* provide

263   *choler* anger

266   *qualification* dilution, appeasement

271   *prosperity* success

277   *That Cassio loves her . . . never seen till used.* See Intro-
-303   duction, p. 18.

280   *constant, loving, noble* (a notable testimonial from an enemy)

284   *accountant* accountable

285   *diet* feed

294   *leash.* Neither 'crush' (Q) nor 'trace' (F) makes good sense. The usual emendation 'trash' (check) is inappropriate to Roderigo, though it, like 'quick hunting', may be ironical. J. Dover Wilson adopts 'leash' from an earlier conjecture.

295   *stand the putting on* do what I incite him to

296   *on the hip* at my mercy

297   *rank garb* gross manner, as a cuckold

II.2   This proclamation is a preparation for the drinking-scene which follows. It was addressed to the audience rather than to a crowd on the stage.

3   *mere* absolute

8   *offices* (for the supply of food and drink)

II.3   This scene is in the guardroom of the castle. The remaining scenes of the play are in or near the castle. Iago engineers the brawl between Roderigo and Cassio - Shakespeare deviates from his source in this respect - and persuades Cassio to appeal to Desdemona for reinstatement.

1, 7   *Michael.* Note the affectionate use of Cassio's Christian name.

7   *with your earliest* at your earliest convenience

9   *the fruits are to ensue* (the marriage has not been consummated)

13-25   *Not this hour . . . She is indeed perfection.* Iago's pruriency about Desdemona is contrasted with Cassio's chaste admiration.

14   *cast* dismissed

21–2 *sounds a parley to provocation* arouses lustful thoughts

27   *stoup* jug

33–4 *I'll drink for you* I'll drink in your place (that is, drink more than my share, to cover your abstemiousness)

36   *qualified* mixed with water

43   *dislikes* displeases

50   *pottle-deep* to the bottom of a two-quart tankard

51   *swelling* lively

52   *hold their honours in a wary distance* are quick to take offence at any suspected insult

53   *elements* quintessence

58   *consequence* what happens
      approve substantiate

60   *rouse* large glass

64–8 *And let me the canakin clink.* See The Songs, p. 237.

64   *canakin* small can

67   *life's but a span.* Compare Psalm 39.5: 'Behold thou hast made my days as it were a span long.'

72   *potting* drinking

77   *Almaine* German

84–91 *King Stephen . . . cloak about thee.* This song was earlier than 1600. See The Songs, p. 238.

84   *and-a.* The syllable was inserted for the sake of the tune.

87   *lown* loon, rogue

96–9 *No, for I hold him to be unworthy . . . souls must not be saved.* Cassio is already drunk, as Shakespeare indicates by his moralizing and theology.

104–5 *The Lieutenant is to be saved before the Ancient.* This is likely to rub salt in Iago's wounds.

108   *my Ancient* (another reference to Cassio's superior rank)

125   *horologe* clock
      a double set twice round

135   *ingraft* ingrafted

143   *twiggen-bottle* bottle cased in wicker-work. This may
       mean (1) beat Roderigo till he resembles wicker-work,
       or (2) chase him through the holes in a wicker-work
       case. The second explanation is more probable.

148   *mazzard* head

155   *Diablo* the Devil

174   *quarter* friendship

176   *unwitted* bereft of their wits. Believers in astrology
       thought that planets could drive men mad (compare
       V.2.111-12).

179   *odds* quarrel

185   *stillness* quietness, sobriety

187   *censure* judgement

189   *rich opinion* high reputation

193   *offends* hurts

200   *collied* blackened

204   *rout* brawl

205   *approved* proved guilty

210   *on the court and guard of safety* in the guard-room, while
       actually members of the watch (who should protect the
       safety of the town)

212   *partially affined* bound by partiality
       leagued in office unwilling to testify against a superior

214-40 *Touch me not so near . . . Which patience could not pass.*
       Iago has the difficult task of persuading both Othello
       and Cassio that he is minimizing the latter's fault, and of
       persuading Montano that he is not doing this.

245   *I'll make thee an example.* This seems to suggest that
       Othello is being severe because his wife has been dis-
       turbed.

247   (stage direction) *Montano is led off.* Both Q and F
       ascribe 'Lead him off' to Othello, but it is probably a
       stage direction.

261-4 *Reputation is an idle and most false imposition . . . repute
       yourself such a loser.* Compare III.3.154-60, where Iago
       says the opposite.

265   *cast* dismissed

267–8 *beat his offenceless dog to affright an imperious lion* punish the innocent to deter the great criminal

271 *slight* worthless

272 *parrot* nonsense

273 *fustian* bombast

284 *applause* desire for applause

295 *Hydra* (snake with many heads slain by Hercules)

298 *ingredience* ingredients

300 *familiar creature* friendly spirit

310 *free* open

314 *splinter* put a splint on

326–52 *And what's he then that says I play the villain . . . That shall enmesh them all.* See Introduction, p. 20.

328 *Probal* reasonable

330 *subdue* persuade

331 *fruitful* generous

333 *renounce his baptism.* The statement is one of several references to Othello's faith.

337 *appetite* desire

338 *function* exercise of faculties

339 *parallel* (to Iago's plot)

340 *Divinity* theology

341 *put on* incite

354 *cry* pack

365–6 *Though other things grow fair against the sun, | Yet fruits that blossom first will first be ripe* the fact that you have already got Cassio dismissed means that you will soon enjoy Desdemona, despite the apparent happiness of her marriage

375 *jump* exactly

III.1 This scene follows soon after the conclusion of Act II, when day was already breaking. It was an Elizabethan custom to awaken a newly married couple with music. The Clown has little individuality and his jests are feeble. It has been argued that Shakespeare did not wish to lower the tension by arousing hearty laughter, but he need not have introduced a clown at all to act as a messenger.

1 *I will content your pains* I will reward you for your trouble

3–4 *have your instruments been in Naples.* This is an allusion to the results of the pox.

8–9 *tail . . . tale* (indecent quibble)

19–20 *for I'll away* (either a snatch of song or a misprint)

23 *quillets* quibbles

30 *In happy time* you come at the right moment

39 *Florentine.* Cassio is surprised that Iago, a Venetian, should be as kind as one of his own fellow-countrymen.

48 *take the safest occasion by the front* seize on the first safe occasion

54 *bosom* heart

III.2 This little scene has two functions – to remind us of Othello's military responsibilities, and to prepare the way for his entrance with Iago in the next scene.

2 *do* convey

3 *works* fortifications

III.3 This is the longest scene in the play. At the beginning, Othello is perfectly happy in his marriage; at the end, he has decided to murder Desdemona and Cassio. Unless we realize the extent to which Shakespeare has telescoped the action, we shall be bound to think that Othello was absurdly prone to jealousy, instead of 'not easily jealous' as he claims at the end of the play. Desdemona's promise to Cassio to get him reinstated is a sign of her innocence and inexperience; not because she has any reason to fear Othello's jealousy, but because in her natural warmth and generosity she does not realize that she is interfering in professional matters.

12 *strangeness* estrangement

15   *nice* thin
16   *breed itself so out of circumstance* be so long delayed
17   *supplied* filled up
19   *doubt* fear
20   *give thee warrant of* guarantee
22   *My lord shall never rest.* Desdemona, however charm-
        ingly, is proposing to nag Othello until she gets her way.
23   *watch him tame* prevent him from sleeping (as hawks
        were tamed)
24   *shrift* confessional
27   *solicitor* advocate
35   *I like not that.* Iago begins his temptation.
47   *present* immediate
67   *check* reprimand
70   *mammering* stammering, hesitating
71   *came a-wooing with you?* This is the first we hear of
        Cassio's part in Othello's wooing and it is difficult to
        reconcile with the Moor's own account in I.3. There are
        four possible explanations: (1) Desdemona supposed
        that Othello was wooing her before he realized it him-
        self; (2) Othello gave a slightly distorted account of the
        events leading up to his declaration; (3) Desdemona is
        referring to the period between the declaration and the
        elopement, though she would hardly dispraise him then;
        (4) Shakespeare wanted to give a lead to Iago's words
        later in the scene (lines 93–4) and did not bother about
        the discrepancy.
74   *bring him in* get him reinstated
79   *peculiar* personal
82   *poise* weight
90   *wretch* (term of endearment)
91   *But I do* if I do not
91-2   *And when I love thee not, | Chaos is come again.* This
        proves to be prophetic.
106   *monster.* Compare line 164.
114   *conceit* idea
119   *stops* pauses

121   *of custom* customary

122   *close dilations* involuntary delays

126   *none* (not to be men)

139   *leets* (days on which courts are held)

146   *of.* The emendation 'oft' for 'of' would improve the syntax but is not really necessary.
        jealousy suspicious nature

148   *conjects* conjectures

150   *scattering* random

154–5   *Good name in man and woman, dear my lord, | Is the immediate jewel of their souls* (proverbial)

155   *immediate* nearest the heart

167–8   *But O, what damnèd minutes tells he o'er, | Who dotes yet doubts, suspects yet fondly loves!* This proves to be Othello's fate.

169   *O misery!* Othello is not referring to himself.

170   *Poor and content is rich, and rich enough* (proverbial)

171   *fineless* boundless

176–7   *To follow still the changes of the moon | With fresh suspicions* indulge in new suspicions several times a month

177–8   *No, to be once in doubt | Is once to be resolved* if I once doubt, I will settle the question one way or the other (compare lines 188–90)

178   *goat* (supposed to be lustful)

180   *exsufflicate and blown* inflated and blown up (but some think the words mean 'spat out and fly-blown')

186   *doubt* suspicion

198   *self-bounty* inherent generosity

200   *In Venice they do let God see the pranks . . . but keep't*
-202   *unknown.* Othello begins to be worried at this point because of his comparative ignorance of Venetian society.

204   *She did deceive her father, marrying you* (echoing Brabantio's last words in I.3)

208   *seel* blind
        oak the grain of oak

211   *I am bound to thee for ever* (with a possible quibble on 'bound')

217   *issues* conclusions

220   *success* result

223   *honest* chaste

227   *affect* like

230-31 *Foh! One may smell in such a will most rank, | Foul dis-
        proportion, thoughts unnatural.* This mention of differ-
        ence of colour is Iago's strongest card. His earlier
        exclamation 'Pish!' (II.1.255) and 'Foh!' here suggest
        there is a streak of puritanism in him.

232   *in position* positively

235   *fall to match* happen to compare
        country country's

236   *happily* maybe

247   *means* (to recover his post)

248   *entertainment* reinstatement

251   *busy* interfering

253   *free* innocent

254   *government* self-control

257   *haggard* wild (a term in falconry)

258   *jesses* straps tied to legs of hawks

260   *prey at fortune* fend for herself. At this point Othello is
        not thinking of killing Desdemona but only of casting
        her off.
        Haply perhaps

261   *soft parts* pleasant arts

262   *chamberers* gallants

267   *toad*. Othello begins to use the characteristic animal
        imagery of Iago.

271   *Prerogatived* privileged

273   *forkèd plague* cuckold's horns

274   *do quicken* are conceived

276   *I'll not believe't*. As soon as he sees Desdemona, Othello
        repudiates Iago's temptation; but the recovery of faith
        is only temporary.

277   *generous* noble

282   *watching* not getting enough sleep

284   *napkin* handkerchief. The loss of the handkerchief is

Shakespeare's invention. In Cinthio's tale it is stolen. (See Introduction, p. 11.) Desdemona forgets the precious love-token because, in her love for Othello, she is concerned about his 'headache'.

293	*ta'en out* copied
296	*fantasy* whim
299	*A thing* (the female pudenda)
313	*import* importance
316	*Be not acknown on't* don't acknowledge anything about it
323	*conceits* ideas
324	*distaste* be distasteful
325	*act* action
327	*poppy* opium (derived from the poppy)
	mandragora narcotic plant
328	*drowsy* causing sleep
330	*owed'st* didst own
337	*free* untroubled
339-40	*He that is robbed, not wanting what is stolen,* | *Let him not know't, and he's not robbed at all* (proverbial)
339	*wanting* missing
343	*Pioners* sappers
344	*So* if
351	*circumstance* pageantry
352	*mortal* deadly
353	*Jove's dread clamours* (thunder)
362	*probation* proof
372	*bu'y* be with
373	*make thine honesty a vice* (by carrying it to excess)
376-7	*I thank you . . . such offence.* The couplet underlines the fact that he is about to exit.
377	*sith* since
379	*should* ought to be (quibbling on 'shouldst' in the previous line)
381	*honest* chaste
384	*Dian* Diana (goddess of chastity)
385-7	*If there be cords or knives,* | *Poison or fire or suffo-*

cating streams, | *I'll not endure it.* Othello is thinking of suicide.

392 *supervisor* looker-on

396 *bolster* share a bolster

400 *prime* lecherous

401 *salt* lustful
pride heat

403 *imputation and strong circumstance* strong circumstantial evidence

425 *foregone conclusion* previous consummation

426 *shrewd doubt* cursed suspicion. This line is given to Othello in F, perhaps rightly.

429 *yet we see nothing done* (referring to Othello's demand for ocular proof)

431 *Have you not sometimes seen a handkerchief.* Iago reserves this 'proof' till Othello is too upset to think clearly.

445 *hearted* seated in the heart

446 *fraught* burden

447 *aspics'* venomous snakes'

450–53 *Like to the Pontic sea . . . and the Hellespont.* The simile, like several others in the play, was derived from Holland's translation of Pliny's *Natural History.* Either it was a late addition to the text, or omitted from Q. Actors would be unlikely to omit the lines.

450 *Pontic sea* Black Sea

453 *Propontic* Sea of Marmora
Hellespont Dardanelles

456 *capable* ample

461 *clip* encompass

463 *execution* activities
wit intelligence

465 *remorse* compassion. Iago means that the utmost cruelty will be reckoned as kindness because he is doing it for Othello.

466 *ever* soever

476 *I am your own* (1) I am your faithful servant; (2) you have become possessed with my spirit

III.4.1–22   *Do you know, sirrah . . . attempt the doing of it.* The feeble quibbling provides some slight relief between the intensity of the previous scene and that which follows.

24   *I know not.* Emilia's lie makes it difficult for her to explain matters after Othello has shown his jealousy.

26   *crusadoes* gold coins

31   *humours* bodily fluids determining temperament

38   *fruitfulness* generosity or amorousness
       liberal generous or licentious

40   *sequester* sequestration, removal

47   *our new heraldry.* Possibly this is a topical reference. The meaning is that people used 'to give their hands and their hearts together, but we think it a finer grace to look asquint, our hand looking one way, and our heart another' (Sir William Cornwallis, 1601).

49   *chuck* (term of endearment)

51   *salt and sorry rheum* wretched running cold

57   *charmer* enchantress

59   *amiable* beloved

63   *fancies* loves

69–72   *there's magic in the web of it . . . prophetic fury sewed the work.* The lines derive from Ariosto, *Orlando Furioso*, XLVI.80.

72   *prophetic fury* 'il furor profetico' (Ariosto)

74   *mummy* preparation made from mummies

79   *rash* rashly

90   *talk* talk to

101   *hungerly* hungrily

104   *happiness* good luck

109   *office* loyal service

117   *shut myself up* confine myself

121   *favour* appearance

124   *blank* centre of target, range

137   *unhatched practice* undisclosed plot

139   *puddled* made muddy

141–4   *'Tis even so . . . that sense | Of pain.* See An Account of the Text, p. 233. Neither Q nor F gives a satisfactory text, but the sense is clear.

146   *bridal* wedding

147   *unhandsome* inadequate

       warrior. Desdemona is thinking of Othello's greeting on his arrival in Cyprus (II.1.176).

151–3 *Pray heaven it be state matters . . . Concerning you.* Emilia is feeling guilty about the handkerchief.

152   *toy* fancy

157   *monster*. Compare III.3.164.

169   *week*. Cassio, according to one time-scheme, arrived in Cyprus only on the previous day; but a week could elapse between III.3 and III.4. This, however, would conflict with Othello's demand at the end of III.3 that Cassio should be killed within three days and with the natural assumption that Othello would demand the handkerchief at the first opportunity.

174   *continuate* uninterrupted

176   *Take me this work out* copy this embroidery for me

197   *circumstanced* give way to circumstance

IV.1   The opening of this scene indicates that despite Othello's determination to kill Desdemona he still loves her; and Iago, knowing that every hour she lives increases his own exposure, is driven to arouse Othello's rage by harping on the sexual relations of Cassio and Desdemona.

9   *So* if

21   *As doth the raven o'er the infected house.* A croaking raven was thought to portend death to the plague-stricken inmates of a house.

25   *abroad* in the world

27   *voluntary dotage* willing infatuation

28   *Convincèd or supplied* overcome or gratified sexually

38–9 *First to be hanged and then to confess!* This impossibility indicates Othello's hopeless confusion of mind.

40   *shadowing* foreshadowing, darkening

40–41 *without some instruction* if there were no basis of fact

41   *shakes* shake

42   *Noses, ears, and lips.* Othello is thinking of the supposed love-making between Cassio and Desdemona.

50-51   *epilepsy.* | *This is his second fit* (possibly an invention)

53   *lethargy* unconsciousness

58   *on great occasion* on an important matter

60   *mock.* Othello thinks Iago is referring to the cuckold's horns.

64   *civil* civilized

67   *May draw with you* (as though they were horned cattle)

68   *unproper* shared with a lover

69   *peculiar* their own alone

71   *lip* kiss
       secure free from suspicion

73   *what I am* (that is, a cuckold)
       what shall be what will be my action (see An Account of the Text, p. 233)

75   *a patient list* bounds of patience

79   *ecstasy* fit

81   *encave* hide

82   *fleers* sneers

86   *cope* meet (with a sexual undertone)

88   *all in all in spleen* quite transformed by passion

92   *keep time* be restrained

94   *housewife* (pronounced 'huzif') hussy

101   *unbookish* ignorant

104   *addition* title

108   *caitiff* wretch

119   *Roman* (referring to Roman triumphs)

120   *customer* harlot

127   *scored* branded

134   *sea-bank* sea-shore

135   *bauble* plaything

142-3 *but not that dog I shall throw it to!* (when he has cut it off)

146   *such another.* This does not imply that Cassio fails to recognize Bianca; it is merely an idiomatic way of referring to a person one knows only too well. Pandarus

commenting on Cressida's bawdy talk in *Troilus and Cressida*, says 'You are such another!'

fitchew polecat, strumpet

(stage direction) The arrival of Bianca with the handkerchief is a stroke of luck which Iago turns to good account.

154   *hobby-horse* harlot

169   *How shall I murder him, Iago? ... You shall hear more by*
-211   *midnight.* This dialogue brings out the conflict between love and jealousy in Othello's mind, 'the struggle not to love her' (Coleridge).

199   *messes* pieces of meat

204   *unprovide* make reluctant

210   *be his undertaker* deal with him

238   *on't* of it

239   *I am glad to see you mad* (to rejoice at your lover's promotion. But possibly 'mad' is an abbreviation of 'madam' and Desdemona is astonished at Othello's cold politeness.)

245   *teem* be impregnated

246   *falls* let fall

252-6   *What would you with her ... And turn again.* Othello is pretending that Desdemona is a harlot and Lodovico a potential client.

259   *passion* grief

265   *Goats and monkeys!* Compare III.3.400.

269   *accident* fate

272   *censure* judgement

276   *use* custom

IV.2   In this scene Othello treats his wife as though she were a prostitute and Emilia as a bawd; but though he accuses Desdemona of adultery, he does not give her a chance of defending herself by naming her supposed lover, her accuser, or the evidence against her.

20   *whore* (Desdemona)

21 *closet lock and key* concealer
26 *Some of your function* do your office
27 *procreants* those engaged in procreation
29 *mystery* trade (of procuress)
42 *motive* cause
46–7 *heaven ... they*. Shakespeare possibly wrote 'God ... he'. See An Account of the Text, p. 231.
53–4 *A fixèd figure for the time of scorn | To point his slow unmoving finger at!* Othello thinks of himself as an object of mockery, pointed at by the scornful time, as the figure on a clock or dial is pointed at by the hand, which moves so slowly that it seems not to move at all.
56 *garnered* stored
61 *gender* engender
    Turn thy complexion change colour
64 *honest* chaste
65 *shambles* butchers' slaughter-house
66 *quicken* receive life
72 *commoner* whore
76 *moon* (symbolizing chastity)
    winks shuts her eyes
82 *vessel* body. Compare 1 Thessalonians 4.3–4: 'that ye should abstain from fornication: That every one of you should know how to possess his vessel in holiness and honour.'
83 *other* of another man
87 *I cry you mercy* I beg your pardon
103 *water* (tears)
107–8 *stick | The smallest opinion on my least misuse* have the least suspicion of my least misbehaviour (Q reads 'greatest abuse': perhaps Shakespeare wrote 'worst misuse')
113 *I am a child to chiding* I have had little experience of chiding
120 *callet* drab
128 *trick* whim, delusion
131 *cogging* deceiving

131   *to get some office.* But Emilia does not suspect Iago.

137   *form* appearance

140   *companions* fellows

143   *within door* less loudly

144   *squire* fellow

146   *suspect me with the Moor.* Compare II.1.286.

147   *go to.* This is an expression with a variety of meanings, here 'be quiet'.

152   *discourse* course

154   *Delighted them* took delight

155   *yet* still

159   *defeat* destroy

162   *addition* title

170   (stage direction) *Enter Roderigo.* On Shakespeare's unlocalized stage, it would not seem that Roderigo had sought out Iago in a private room of the castle.

175   *daff'st* dost put me off

177   *conveniency* opportunity

188   *a votarist* a nun, vowed to chastity

189   *sudden respect* immediate notice

191-2 *go to.* See note to IV.2.147. Iago's use of the expression is probably accompanied by an obscene gesture. Roderigo means he cannot have sexual intercourse with Desdemona.

194   *fopped* duped

203   *intendment* intention

216   *engines for* plots against

225   *determinate* conclusive

232   *harlotry* harlot

240   *high* fully

V.3   Now the time of Desdemona's murder approaches Othello has recovered his self-control. The song is omitted from the Q text probably because the boy who played Desdemona could no longer sing. But some critics think the song was added later.

11   *incontinent* forthwith

19   *checks* rebukes

22   *All's one* all right

26   *mad* faithless

30-31   *I have much to do | But* I find it difficult not

33   *night-gown* dressing-gown

34   *proper* handsome

38-54   *The poor soul sat sighing ... you'll couch with moe men.*
        This is adapted from an old song in which the forsaken
        lover is a man. See The Songs, p. 239.

38   *sycamore* fig mulberry (not the modern sycamore)

39   *willow* (an emblem of forsaken love)

45   *these* (necklace, jewels or other ornaments)

54   *moe* more

58-104 *Dost thou in conscience think ... but by bad mend!* This
        dialogue brings out the difference between Desdemona's
        innocence and idealism and Emilia's worldly-wise
        cynicism and realism.

62   *heavenly light* the moon

67-8   *it is a great price for a small vice.* The rhyme suggests
        that it is meant to be a quotation.

71-2   *joint ring* ring made in two separate parts

73   *exhibition* gift, allowance

74   *Ud's* God's

83   *to th'vantage* in addition

84   *store* populate

85   *But I do think it is their husbands' faults.* Emilia, who
        has been speaking in prose, now drops into verse, to
        give her words a kind of choric tone.

86   *duties.* Emilia is probably referring to sexual duties and
        to Iago.

87   *foreign* other than their wives'

88   *peevish jealousies.* This could refer to Iago or Othello.

90   *having* allowance
        in despite out of spite

91   *galls* spirits to resent

103   *uses* habits

212

104   *Not to pick bad from bad, but by bad mend* not to get worse through evil chance or suffering but to learn from it

V.1   Iago, characteristically, gets Roderigo to attack Cassio, though he has to intervene himself; but he fails to kill either Cassio or Roderigo. Even without Emilia's evidence he would be ruined.

1   *bulk* projecting part of building. On the Elizabethan stage Roderigo would hide behind the pillar supporting the canopy.

2   *bare* unsheathed

5   *resolution* (pronounced with five syllables)

10   *'Tis but a man gone.* Roderigo is quoting Iago.
Forth my sword! He dies! He is rehearsing the murder in his mind.

11   *I have rubbed this young quat almost to the sense* I have rubbed this pimple almost to the quick

16   *bobbed* swindled

19–20   *He hath a daily beauty in his life | That makes me ugly.* Cassio is handsome and popular. It is significant that Iago should confess that his envy is a more important motive than the danger that Othello would have it out with Cassio.

25   *coat* (coat of mail, or leather jerkin)

27   (stage direction) *above* on the balcony

29   *It is even so.* Othello either mistakes Roderigo's voice for Cassio's and agrees that he is a villain, or else he continues his previous speech.

34–6   *And your unblest fate hies . . . with lust's blood be spotted.* Neither F nor Q is satisfactory and some critics think the lines were interpolated. It is odd that Othello should speak of 'lust's blood' when he has decided to strangle or smother Desdemona.

36   (stage direction) *Enter Lodovico and Gratiano.* Gratiano has just arrived with news of Brabantio's death.

37   *passage* passers-by
42   *heavy* gloomy, dark
44   *come in to* approach
69   *I cry you mercy* pardon me
98   *that's well said* well done!
101   *Save you your labour.* Bianca is tending Cassio.
106   *gastness* frightened look
122–3 *of life as honest | As you that thus abuse me.* Bianca is per-
       haps more honest, in one sense of the word, than Emilia.
129   *fordoes* undoes

V.2   The bed was probably pushed forward from the cur-
       tained space under the balcony, as otherwise much of
       the action would be invisible to part of the audience
       It has often been observed that Othello has recovered
       something of his nobility at the beginning of this scene,
       but in his 'darkened reason' he believes he is sacrificing
       his wife to an ideal rather than committing a brutal
       murder. The actual deed, however, is committed not
       calmly but in a blind fury when Desdemona weeps for
       Cassio.

1   *cause* (adultery)
4   *whiter skin of hers than snow* her skin whiter than snow
7   *light . . . light* (1) the torch; (2) Desdemona's life
8   *flaming minister* serviceable torch. Compare Psalm
       104.4: 'He maketh his angels spirits and his ministers
       a flame of fire.'
12   *Promethean.* Prometheus brought fire to men.
13   *relume* relight
22   *It strikes where it doth love.* Compare Hebrews 12.6:
       'For whom the Lord loveth, he chasteneth.'
38   *When your eyes roll so.* This description was probably
       necessary on the Jacobean stage, where there was no
       artificial lighting. Compare line 43 below.
40   *They are loves I bear to you* (in deceiving her father)
47   *will – so.* There is a pause between these two words
       while Desdemona controls herself.

52   *presently* at once
55   *conception* belief
59   *Offend* wrong
63   *stone* turn to stone
73   *ta'en order* taken steps
83   *Being done, there is no pause* now the deed is begun, I cannot stop
85   *O Lord, Lord, Lord!* Desdemona tries to pray; and Emilia's words in the next line seem like a macabre echo.
90   *So, so.* As suffocated persons do not recover consciousness, some actors and critics make Othello stab Desdemona. But Shakespeare may have been ignorant or, as some medical authorities suggest, Desdemona may die of shock.
94   *high* loud
99   *O, insupportable! O heavy hour!* Othello already repents.
102   *yawn* (with an earthquake)
       alteration (the change brought about by Desdemona's death)
105   *curtains* (of the bed, to hide the body)
110   *error* straying off course
125   *I myself.* Desdemona's lie, oddly condemned by some critics, is a final proof of her loving heart.
130   *She's like a liar gone to burning hell.* It has been suggested that Othello's violent repudiation of the lie indicates that he subconsciously realizes that if she had been unfaithful she would not have lied to save him.
131   *O, the more angel she.* Emilia's love for Desdemona leads her to risk her life, and finally to lose it. She is credibly transformed from the cynical spokesman of worldly wisdom at the end of the previous scene.
144   *chrysolite* (a semi-precious stone)
149   *iterance* repetition
150   *made mocks with love* used love as a plaything (referring either to Desdemona's love for Othello, or to her friendly intervention on behalf of Cassio)
182   *charm your tongue* be silent

191   *I thought so then.* This is a reference either to IV.2.129 or to her misgiving when Iago takes the handkerchief.

206   *turn* deed

208   *reprobance* (the state of damnation)

211   *A thousand times.* This, obviously, could not have happened during the course of the play, even when every allowance has been made for 'double time'; but Othello may be vaguely referring to the period before and after his marriage.

212   *gratify* reward

213   *recognizance* token

216   *My father gave my mother.* But earlier (III.4.55–6) Othello has told Desdemona that the handkerchief was given to his mother by an Egyptian. The discrepancy is probably an oversight, and could be resolved by the assumption that Othello's father purchased the handkerchief from the Egyptian. But some critics implausibly suggest that the earlier account was invented by Othello to frighten Desdemona.

218   *liberal* unrestrainedly
       north (north wind)

231   *coxcomb* fool

232–3   *Are there no stones in heaven | But what serve for the thunder?* (to punish such wickedness)

237   *notorious* notable

242   *whipster* one who whips out his sword (though Montano, an experienced soldier, hardly deserves the description)

243   *why should honour outlive honesty?* why should reputation outlive desert?

251   *ice-brook's.* The sword was tempered by plunging it into icy water. (It has been argued that 'Isebrookes' – the reading of Q – is a spelling of Innsbruck's; but the definite article makes this impossible.)

256   *naked* unarmed

262   *stop* power to stop me

265   *butt* goal

266   *sea-mark* beacon

268   *Man* wield

271   *compt* Judgement day

272–3   *This look of thine will hurl my soul from heaven | And fiends will snatch at it.* Othello recognizes that he is damned.

275   *slave.* Othello is speaking of himself, not of Iago.

283   *fable* (that a devil has cloven feet)

289   *practice* plot
        slave villain

291   *An honourable murderer, if you will* (spoken, presumably, with bitter irony)

294   *consent* agree

296   *Dear.* The epithet shows Cassio's noble forgiveness as well as his love for Othello.

310   *discontented* full of discontent

313   *in the nick* (of time)

317   *confessed.* Iago is willing to confess his deeds, but not his motives.

323   *cast* dismissed

330   *hold him long* keep him long alive

334   *Soft you* one moment

337   *unlucky* unfortunate

342   *Perplexed* bewildered

343   *Indian.* There are many stories of Indians throwing away precious stones: but the F reading, 'Iudean', also makes good sense if it is taken to refer to Judas. Compare line 355.

344   *subdued eyes* overcome by grief, weeping

347   *med'cinable gum* (myrrh, 'associated with incense, and therefore atonement and sacrifice' – A. Walker)

353   *period* ending

357   *Spartan dog* (notorious for their fierceness)

358   *fell* deadly

362   *seize upon* take legal possession of

363   *Lord Governor* (Cassio)

364   *censure* trial

AN ACCOUNT OF THE TEXT

Othello was first published in 1622, some eighteen years after its first performance, in an edition known as the Quarto (Q). In the following year the play was included in the First Folio (F), the collected edition of Shakespeare's plays. The F text was partly based on that of Q (or on the transcript from which it was printed) and partly on a copy of the Prompt Book. As both Q and F omit passages, a modern editor has to make use of both. What things caused the divergences are still a matter of debate. Omissions in Q may be due to the transcriber or the compositors, and some of them may rather be due to revisions of the original play (see Coghill below). Omissions in F include the deletion of many oaths in order to comply with the new regulations about profanity; others may be due to the carelessness of the book-keeper who had the job of collating the manuscript with the Prompt Book. It was probably a rushed job. As some mistakes are common to Q and F, there may well be others impossible to detect.

We may agree with Alice Walker's attack on the Q text (*Shakespeare Survey 5*, 1952; *Textual Problems of the First Folio*, 1953; and her edition of the play, 1957) but she exaggerates its faults, blaming them on the book-keeper 'who saved himself time and trouble by using his memory rather than his eyes'. Nevill Coghill in *Shakespeare's Professional Skills* (1964) argues convincingly that the poet revised the play so as to eliminate weaknesses which had struck him in performance. Roderigo's speech (I.i.123 ff) clarifies the situation for the audience; the Pontic Sea simile enormously increases the effectiveness of the temptation scene – but this might well be due to careless omission by the transcriber; there are several passages inserted to arouse sympathy for Emilia (e.g. IV.iii.85–102). In *The Stability of Shakespeare's Text* (1965), E. A. J. Honigmann argued that Shakespeare, like other poets, introduced variants while copying out his own work; and in a later article in *The Library* (June 1982), without abandoning this theory, he agreed with Coghill that Shakespeare deliberately revised the play. This hypothesis is acted upon by the editors of the Oxford *Complete Works* (1986) and is discussed in *William Shakespeare: A Textual Companion* (by Stanley Wells, Gary Taylor, et al., Oxford, 1987).

In my own article on the text of *Othello*, written while I was working on this edition, and published in *Shakespeare Studies I* (1965), I argued that although an editor should use F as his copy-text, there are scores of Q readings which are manifestly superior, and that it is necessary to deviate from F in approximately 300 places, and that in 200 of them Q should be accepted. When both Q and F are unsatisfactory it is necessary to amend. Every variant must be judged on its merits rather than on the assumption that we should wherever possible follow F. The collations that follow show how much these principles have been applied.

COLLATIONS

1

Passages Omitted in Quarto

I.1.	122–38	If't ... yourself
I.2.	20	Which, when I know
	65	If ... bound
	72–7	Judge ... attach thee
I.3.	16	By Signor Angelo
	24–30	For ... profitless
	63	Being ... sense
	118	The ... you
	123	I ... blood

I.3. 192 Which ... heart
      273 her
      274 it
      280 So
      308 O villainous
    345-6 She must change for youth
    357-8 if ... issue
      376 I'll sell all my land
II.1. 39-40 Even ... regard
       63 quirks of
      112 DESDEMONA
      154 See ... behind
      234 Why, none; why, none
      237 a devilish knaue
      246 Blessed pudding
      248 that I did
      249 obscure
      252 Villainous thoughts, Roderigo
      254 master and
      255 Pish
II.2.   9 of feasting
II.3. 67 O
       96 to be
     98-9 and ... saued
      112 Why
      184 to
      245 dear
      297 O, strange
III.1. 54 CASSIO I am much bound to you
III.3. 163 OTHELLO Ha
    380-87 By ... satisfied
    450-57 Iago ... heauen
      465 in me
III.4.8-10 CLOWN To ... this
       98 of it
      179 Well, well
    191-2 BIANCA ... not

2

Passages Omitted in Folio

III.3. 178   once
      183   well
      221   at
      421   then
      449   perhaps
III.4. 22   of
      37   yet
      84   sir
      90   OTHELLO ... Cassio
IV.1. 52   No, forbear
     103   now
     110   a
     120   her
     124   shall
  135–6   by this hand
     248   an
IV.2. 32   But not the words
     80   Impudent strumpet
    166   And ... you
    187   to
    227   of
IV.3. 20   in them
     23   thee
     71   it
 V.2. 52   Yes
     85   DESDEMONA O Lord, Lord, Lord
    143   Nay
    239   here
    334   him

3

Readings Accepted from Quarto, with Rejected Folio Reading

I.1. 25   togèd] Tongued
    30   Christian] Christen'd
    67   full] fall
        thick-lips] Thicks-lips
   101   bravery] knauerie

I.1. 104 them] their
      147 produced] producted
      183 night] might

I.2.   10 pray] pray you
       15 and] or
       16 That] The
       21 provulgate] promulgate
       68 darlings] Deareling
       84 Where] Whether

I.3.   1 these] this
        4 and forty] forty
       35 injointed] inioynted them
       45 wish] to
       93 proceedings] proceeding
       99 maimed] main'd
      107 overt] ouer
      122 till] tell
      129 fortunes] Fortune
      138 travels'] Trauellours
      140 and hills] Hills
           heads] head
      141 the] my
      142 other] others
      144 Do grow] Grew
           This] These things
      146 thence] hence
      154 intentively] instinctively
      158 sighs] kisses
      182 lord of all my] the Lord of
      217 ear] eares
   237–8 If ... father's.] Why at her Fathers?
      239 Nor I: I would not] Nor would I
      244 you? Speak.] you Desdemona?
      245 did love] loue
      254 which] why
      265 For] When
      267 instruments] Instrument

I.3. 274-5 You ... night] *Sen.* You must away to night
279 With] And
296 matters] matter
306 we have] haue we
310 a man] man
327 our (*after* stings)] or
338-9 be ... continue] be long that Desdemona should
continue
345 acerbe as the] bitter as
347 error] errors
389 ear] eares
II.1. 11 banning] foaming
19 they] to
33 prays] praye
34 heaven] Heauens
42 arrivance] Arriuancie
43 this] the
70 clog] enclogge
92 the sea] sea
94 their] this
104 list] leaue
155 wight] wightes
171 an] and
208 hither] thither
217-18 And will she] To
221 again] a game
230 eminently] eminent
235 finder out of occasions] finder of occasion
236 has] he's
253 mutualities] mutabilities
290 for wife] for wift
297 rank] right
II.3. 37 unfortunate] infortunate
75 expert] exquisite
124 the prologue] his prologue
152 God's will] Alas
156 God's ... hold] Fie, fie Lieutenant

II.3.	157	You will be shamed] You'le be asham'd
	159	death] death. He dies
	227	the] then
	234	can I not] cannot I
	259	thought] had thought
	265	ways] more wayes
	292	not so] not
	305	I'll] I
	344	fortunes] Fortune
	352	enmesh] en-mash
	367	By th'mass] Introth
	374	the while] a while
III.1.	21	hear] heare me
III.3.	4	case] cause
	16	circumstance] Circumstances
	39	sneak] steale
	60	or] on
	66	their] her
	74	By'r Lady] Trust me
	105	By ... me] Alas, thou eccho'st me
	106	his] thy
	111	In] Of
	134	free to] free
	137	a breast] that breast
	138	But some] Wherein
	139	session] Sessions
	148	conjects] conceits
	180	blown] blow'd
	196	eye] eyes
	200	God] Heauen
	213	In faith] Trust me
	215	my] your
	231	disproportion] disproportions
	246	to hold him] to him
	256	qualities] Quantities
	270	of] to
	274	Desdemona] Look where she

III.3. 275 O ... mocks] Heauen mock'd
       299 A] You haue a
       308 faith] but
       335 of] in
       337 well] well, fed well
       370 defend] forgiue
       383 Her] My
       390 I] and I
       392 supervisor] super-vision
       422 Over ... sighed ... kissed] ore ... sigh ... kisse
       423 Cried] cry
       426 'Tis ... dream] *Given to Othello*
       429 but] yet
       444 thy hollow cell] the hollow hell
III.4.   5 one] me
            is] 'tis
        23 that] the
        54 faith ... That is] indeed ... That's
        64 wive] Wiu'd
        67 lose] loose't
        94 I'faith] Insooth
        95 Zounds] Away
       133 can he be] is he
       143 that] a
       159 that] the
       167 I'faith] Indeed
       183 by my faith] in good troth
       184 sweet] neither
IV.1.   9 So] If
        21 infected] infectious
        37 confession] Confessions
        45 , work] workes
        60 No] not
        77 unsuiting] resulting F; vnfitting Q (*uncorrected state*)
        79 scuse] scuses
        98 refrain] restraine

227

IV.1. 107 power] dowre
111 i'faith] indeed
124 Faith] Why
131 beckons] becomes
139 hales] shakes
152 not know] know not
162 street] streets
191 a thousand, thousand times] a thousand, a thousand times
214 Come . . . him] this, comes from the Duke. See, your wife's with him
216 Senators] the Senators
238 By my troth] Trust me
278 this] his
281 denote] deonte

IV.2. 23 Pray] Pray you
29 Nay] May
30 knees] knee
54 unmoving] and mouing
91 keep] keepes
116 As . . . bear] That . . . beare it
125 all] and
140 heaven] Heauens
147 O good] Alas
154 in] or
169 stay] staies
223 takes] taketh

IV.3. 12 He] And
17 I would] I, would
22 faith] Father
24 those] these
74 Ud's pity] why

V.1. 1 bulk] Barke
25 think'st] know'st
35 Forth] For
38 cry] voyce
42 It is a] 'Tis

228

V.1. 49 Did] Do
      50 heaven's] heauen
      60 here] there
      90 O heaven] Yes, 'tis
      93 you] your
    104 out o'th'] o'th'
    111 'Las ... What's] Alas, what is ... what is
    116 fruit] fruits
    123 Foh! Fie] Fie

V.2. 15 it] thee
      19 this] that's
      32 heaven] Heauens
      35 say so] say
      57 Then Lord] O Heauen
    102 Should] Did
    118 O Lord] Alas
    151 that she] she
    227 steal it] steal't
    249 I die, I die] alas, I dye
    289 damnèd] cursed
    292 did I] I did
    312 to have] t'haue
    313 nick] interim
    314 the] thou
    317 but] it but
    343 Indian] Iudean

4

Some Rejected Quarto Variants

I.1. 33 Moorship's] Worships
      39 affined] assign'd
      66 daws] Doues
      73 chances ... on't] changes ... out
    141 thus deluding you] this delusion
    146 place] pate
    166 she deceives] thou deceiuest
    173 maidhood] manhood

I.2. 22   siege] height

41   sequent] frequent

46   hath sent about] sent aboue

I.3. 6   the aim] they aym'd

122   truly] faithfull

138   portance in] with it all

165   hint] heate

175   on my head] lite on me

246   storm] scorne

248   very quality] vtmost pleasure

257   Let ... voice] Your voyces Lords: beseech you let her will | Have a free way

266   Of ... seel] And ... foyles

I.3. 267   officed] actiue

271   estimation] reputation

280   import] concerne

289   if thou hast eyes] haue a quicke eye

347   Therefore] shee must haue change, she must. Therefore

362   conjunctive] communicatiue

387   plume] make

II.1. 8   mountains melt on them] the huge mountaine meslt

12   chidden] chiding

15   ever-fixèd] euer fired

20   lads] Lords

68   high] by

72   mortal] common

80   Make ... in] And swiftly come to

95   See for the news] So speakes this voyce

167   gyve] catch

179   calms] calmenesse

235   slipper and subtle] subtle slippery

286   lusty] lustfull

II.3. 51   else] lads

129   Prizes the virtue] Praises the vertues

143   twiggen-bottle] wicker bottle

II.3. 187   mouths] men

       200   collied] coold

       313   broken joint] braule

     357–8   and so ... Venice] as that comes to, and no money
                 at all, and with that wit returne to Venice

III.1. 41   sure] soone

III.2.   2   senate] State

III.3. 70   mammering] muttering

       114   conceit] counsell

       122   dilations] denorements

       124   be sworn] presume

       153   What dost thou mean] Zouns

       352   rude] wide

       353   dread clamours] great clamor

       358   mine] mans

       373   lov'st] liuest

       463   execution] excellency

III.4. 51   sorry] sullen

       62   loathèd] lothely

       145   observancy] obseruances

       174   continuate] conuenient

IV.1. 80   return] retire

       82   fleers] Ieeres

      213   I ... Lodovico] Something from Venice sure,
                 tis Lodouico

IV.2. 17   their wives] her sex

       46   I have lost] Why I haue left

       47   they rained] he ram'd

      169   The ... meat] And the great Messengers of Venice
                 stay

      190   acquaintance] acquittance

      207   exception] conception

      232   harlotry] harlot

IV.3. 103   uses] vsage

V.1.   7   stand] sword

        8   deed] dead

       11   quat] gnat

V.1.   14   gain] game
       34   unblest fate hies] fate hies apace
       76   my sweet Cassio, | O Cassio, Cassio, Cassio]
            O my sweete Cassio! | Cassio, Cassio
       86   be ... injury] beare a part in this
      105   gentlemen] Gentlewoman
      106   gastness] ieastures
V.2.   10   thy light] thine
       13   relume] returne
       15   needs must] must needes
       55   conception] conceit
       70   hath used thee] hath – vds death
      111   nearer] neere the
      149   iterance] iteration
      208   reprobance] reprobation
      217   'Twill ... peace?] 'Twill out, 'twill, I hold my
            peace sir, no.
      218   I will speak as ... north] Ile be in speaking ... ayre
      285   Wrench] wring
      347   med'cinable] medicinal
      359   loading] lodging

5

Emendations

I.1.   30   leed] be-leed F; led Q
      152   stand] stands Q , F
      155   hell pains] hell apines F; hells paines Q
I.2.   11   For be assured] Be assur'd F; For be sure Q
       50   carack] Carract F; Carrick Q
I.3.   58   yet] it Q , F
       87   feats of broil] Feats of Broiles F; feate of broyle Q
      177   company] noble company Q , F
      217   piecèd] pierced Q , F
      228   couch] Cooch Q ; Coach F
      232   war] Warres Q , F
      261   In me] In my Q , F

I.3. 323   beam] ballance Q ; braine F
     336   thou these] thou the F; these Q
II.1. 13   mane] Maine Q , F
       65   tire the ingener] tyre the Ingeniuer F; beare all
            excellency Q
       67   He's] He has Q ; Ha's F
       70   enscarped] ensteep'd F; enscerped Q
      108   of doors] of doore F; adores Q
      195   let's] let vs Q , F
      294   I leash] I trace F; I crush Q
II.2.   5   addiction] addition F; minde Q
II.3. 112 well] well then Q , F
      121   in him] him in Q , F
      161   sense of place] place of sense Q , F
      212   leagued] league Q , F
      221   following] following him Q , F
      260   of sense] sence F; offence Q
      308   denotement] deuotement Q , F
III.1. 25 General's wife] Ceneral's wife Q ; General F
III.2.   6 We'll] Well F; We Q
III.3. 119 affright me more] fright me the more F; affright me
            the more Q
      147   that ... then] that your wisedome F; I intreate you
            then Q
      168   fondly] soundly F; strongly Q
      180   exsufflicate] exufflicate Q , F
      182   fair, loves] faire, feeds well, loues Q , F
      202   keep't] kept F; keepe Q
      209   to] too Q , F
      347   make] makes Q , F
      403   circumstance] circumstances Q , F
      437   any that] any it Q , F
      452   feels] keepes F
III.4. 42 there's] heere's Q , F
       82   an] and Q , F
      112   sorrow] sorrowes Q , F
      143   Our] our other Q , F

IV.1. 73   shall] she shall Q , F

        87   gestures] ieasture Q , F

     101   construe] conster Q ; conserue F

     123   win] winnes Q , F

IV.2. 63   Ay, there] I heere Q , F

        79   hear it] hear't Q , F

     167   It is so] It is but so F; Tis but so Q

     175   daff'st] dafts F; doffts Q

IV.3. 38   sighing] singing F

V.1. 22   But ... hear] But so ... heard F; be't so ... hear Q

     114   quite] quite dead F; dead Q

V.2. 107   murder] Murthers Q , F

     216   O God! O heavenly Powers] Oh Heauen! Oh
            heauenly Powres F; O God, O heauenly God Q

     233   serve] serues Q , F

     288   wast] wert Q ; was F

     346   Drop] Drops Q , F

6

Stage Directions

I.1. 82   above] F; at a window Q

     145   Exit above] Exit F; *not in* Q

     160   in his night-gown] *not in* F

I.2. 33   Enter ... torches] Enter Cassio, with Torches F;
            Enter Cassio with lights, Officers and Torches Q
            (both at line 27)

     49   *not in* Q , F

     53   *not in* Q , F

I.3. 0   Enter Duke, Senators, and Officers] F; Enter
            Duke, and Senators set at a Table, with lights
            and Attendants Q

     121   Exit ... attendants] Exit two or three Q; *not in* F

     291   Exeunt ... attendants] Exit F; Exeunt Q

     297   Exeunt . . . Desdemona] Exit Moore and Des-
            demona Q ; Exit F

II.1. 55   Salvo] *not in* F; A shot Q

     82   and attendants] *not in* Q , F

II.1. 99 He kisses Emilia] *not in* Q , F
121 (aside)] *not in* Q , F
164 (aside)] *not in* Q , F
173 Trumpet] Trumpets within Q ; *not in* F
174 (aloud)] *not in* Q , F
191 They kiss] *not in* F
206 Exeunt . . . Roderigo] Exit Q ; Exit Othello and Desdemona F

II.3. 11 and attendants] *not in* Q , F
59 and servants with wine] *not in* Q , F
132 Exit Roderigo] *not in* F
139 Cry within] *not in* F
145 He strikes Roderigo] *not in* Q , F
154 Bell rings] *not in* Q , F
247 Montano is led off] Lead him off Q , F
251 Exeunt . . . Cassio] Exit Moore, Desdemona, and attendants Q ; Exit F

III.3. 239 going] *not in* Q , F
284 He . . . it] *not in* Q , F
312 snatching it] *not in* Q , F

III.4. 34 (Aside)] *not in* Q , F

IV.1. 43 He falls] Falls in a Traunce F ; he fals downe Q
58 Exit Cassio] *not in* Q , F
92 Othello retires] *not in* Q , F
109, 112, 114 etc. (aside)] *not in* Q , F
168 Exit Cassio] *not in* F
169 (coming forward)] *not in* Q , F
212 Trumpet sounds] *not in* Q , F
216 He . . . letter] *not in* Q , F
217 He . . . letter] *not in* Q , F
240 He strikes her] *not in* Q , F
262 Exit Desdemona] *not in* Q , F

IV.2. 89 (Calling)] *not in* Q , F

IV.3. 9 Othello . . . attendants] *not in* Q , F
38 etc. (sings)] *not in* Q , F
44 etc. (She speaks)] *not in* Q , F

V.1. 7 He retires] *not in* Q , F

V.1. 26 'He wounds Roderigo] *not in* Q , F

Iago ... exit] *not in* Q , F

27 above] *not in* Q , F

46 with a light] *not in* F

61 He stabs Roderigo] *not in* Q , F

62 He faints] *not in* Q , F

64 Lodovico ... forward] *not in* Q , F

98 Enter ... chair] *not in* Q , F

104 Cassio ... removed] *not in* Q , F

110 Enter Emilia] *not in* F

128 (Aside)] *not in* Q , F

V.2. 0 with a light] *not in* F

Desdemona in her bed] *not in* Q

15 He kisses her] *not in* F

85 smothers] Q ; stifles F

106 (He unlocks door)] *not in* Q , F

120 She ... curtains] *not in* Q , F

197 (falling on bed)] Oth. fals on the bed Q; *not in* F

199 (rising)] *not in* Q , F

233 He ... exit] *not in* F; The Moore runnes at Iago.
Iago kils his wife Q

249 She dies] *not in* F

269 He goes to the bed] *not in* Q , F

279 in a chair] *not in* F

352 He stabs himself] *not in* F

355 falls on the bed and] *not in* Q , F

361 The ... drawn] *not in* Q , F

THE SONGS

For a full discussion see *Music in Shakespearean Tragedy* by F. W. Sternfeld (1963), from whose work the following notes are, with his permission, derived.

1. 'And let me the canakin clink' (II.3.64).
The tune for this song is not certainly known, but the following tune called 'A Soldier's Life' fits the words. It appears to be traditional, though not printed until 1651 (in John Playford's *The English Dancing Master*). A version of it is familiar as the tune to which, according to stage tradition, Ophelia sings 'Tomorrow is St Valentine's Day' in *Hamlet* (IV.5.46).

2. 'King Stephen was and-a worthy peer' (II.3.84).

A song with the refrain 'Then take thy auld cloak about thee'
is found in the eighteenth century and the music may be a
version of that used for this well-known ballad in Shakespeare's
time. The tune was first printed in James Oswald's *Caledonian
Pocket Companion* (mid eighteenth century); and the following
vocal version appeared in Robert Bremner's *Thirty Scots Songs
for a Voice and Harpsichord* (1757, as revised in 1770).

3. 'The poor soul sat sighing by a sycamore tree' (IV.3.38).
This song was well known. Different settings appear in manuscripts of the sixteenth century and later. The following, which is the only one for voice and lute, seems to be the version most easily adjusted to the words in Shakespeare's text. It is found in a manuscript in the British Museum (Add MSS. 15117, folio 18) dated 1616 or earlier.

1. The poor soul sat sigh-ing, by a sy-ca-more tree, Sing all a green wil-low; Her hand on her bo-som, her head on her knee, Sing wil-low, wil-low, wil-low, wil-low; sing wil-low, wil-low, wil-low, wil-low must be my gar-land. Sing all a green wil-low; wil-low, wil-low, wil-low, sing all a green wil-low must be my gar-land.

2. The fresh streams ran by her and mur-mured her moans; Her salt tears fell from her and sof-tened the stones,

3. Let no-bo-dy blame him; his scorn I ap-prove; If I court moe wo-men, you'll couch with moe men.

4. I called my love false love, but what said he then?

READ MORE IN PENGUIN